THE MISTS

a novella by

Barbara de la Cuesta

Finishing Line Press
Georgetown, Kentucky

THE MISTS

Publisher: Leah Huete de Maines

Editor: Christen Kincaid

Cover Art: Barbara de la Cuesta

Author Photo: Connie Pilling

Cover Design: Elizabeth Maines McCleavy

Order online: www.finishinglinepress.com
also available on amazon.com

Author inquiries and mail orders:
Finishing Line Press
P. O. Box 1626
Georgetown, Kentucky 40324
U. S. A.

At Las Brumas, the clouds came down over the mountain evenings and didn't rise till eleven the next morning, leaving tatters of the mists caught in the coffee bushes.

I

The Rent Thrown in

It was a portent, of course, that things would differently from their plan to drive in Willi's old Buick from Chicago to his uncle's farm in El Salvador.

They were passing through the small city of Querétaro in central Mexico, and Blanche, at the wheel, had just put the Alberto and Inez tape into the player:

"*Alberto presenta a su amiga Clara en el lobby del Hotel:*

"'*Encantadísimo en conocerle,*' *dice Alberto. 'Les invito a un sorbete.*'"

"'*Encan ta di si mo!*'"yelped Blanche.

"It's the superlative," Carl said. "I am most enchanted…"

"Jesus, Carl, the world is all going to hell and people can still say things like that," Blanche was commenting when she cut a corner too sharply and sideswiped an ancient Pontiac parked near a little plaza.

"Oh, my God!" yelled Willi. "Didn't you see it?"

"Yeah, I saw it, Willi. I just still happened to run into it. Look at it; it's a piece of junk." Blanche was laughing, then she was crying.

On the scene immediately was a scruffy soldier; or perhaps he was a policeman; the uniform suggested either. He instructed them to come with him and went round a corner to an armory. There, he took Blanche's license and all of their passports. Then he told them to wait there, and went inside. Willi followed. There was no one at the desk or anywhere else in sight.

They were at lunch, the man said. He took up a post at the door and Willi went back and sat in the car. Suppose they just took off, Carl suggested.

He had their passports and Blanche's license, Willi reminded him.

An hour went by, a good part of another. Blanche didn't think he was really a cop, or a soldier either. But the harm was done.

"If anyone official comes, we can report him," Carl said, but Willi reminded him the man had seen the accident.

Then a well-dressed man came out of the café, and introduced himself as Sr. Areátegui and told them they must pay the man something.

"A very old car," Willi argued. "Many scratches already."

"Five hundred dollars should be enough," said Sr. Areátegui.

"Dollars!" laughed Blanche. "Dollars!"

"I'm afraid so. It is unfortunate."

"Damned unfortunate," said Willi. Carl fished in the backpacks and came up with the money in tens and twenties. It was more than half of the money they had saved since the previous January.

They slept under the stars that night, saving on hotels. Carl lay awake listening to the farm animals stamp their feet in a nearby stable. They were almost fifteen hundred miles from home, from the duplex on Chicago's west side, from his childhood bedroom where a month ago he had lain on his narrow bunk bed with Blanche listening to the Alberto and Inez tapes, from the little Congregational college founded by his great great grandfather where all Browns studied, from the Art Institute where he had met Willi, from the upstairs room with the rooting begonias where he and Willi drank beer and listened to Fidel Castro on short wave.

Here are, the three of us, he thought, who didn't even know each other a year ago: Carl Brown, Blanche Bell, Willi Ott, on the road in Willi's twelve-year old Buick. Going to crash with an uncle of Willi's who owned a sausage factory in Salvador.

Blanche, who it must be admitted was simply along for the ride, lay next to him in her sleeping bag. Actually her bag was spread open because of the heat. Blanche, who had been on the road since she was sixteen and whose last residence before Carl's bedroom had been Boston Common, felt easy under the stars and wanted him to make love to her, but Carl felt too exposed in this field with the cattle stamping nearby. Willi was quite angry with her on this night because of the accident, but chiefly because Blanche had laughed about it. Carl understood her laughter as more of a nervous habit than what Willi considered her making light of most everything in the world. It was a kind of dissolution, her laugh. But he also felt a little sore. Finally she fell asleep.

He, however, couldn't turn off his thoughts and kept shining the flashlight on his watch as the hours went by.

The farm in El Salvador—besides the sausage factory, Willi's uncle raised honeybees and anthuriums—was a little harder to believe in lying here in this field than it had been in the upstairs room in the house on Waltemath Street where they listened to Fidel Castro. In his night thoughts Carl began to doubt they would ever reach that destination, more than six hundred miles from where they were sleeping. Their manner of traveling left them too open to interventions of fate, like today's bit of bad luck. Of course the next bit of luck could be a bit better. Luck was a lady, he'd heard. When he wasn't so sore at her, he could acknowledge that the dismal years in the duplex after his father left them, the years his mother sobs were audible in the night through the thin walls, had been suddenly lightened with the advent of Blanche, like a summer storm. Something good could happen next.

Yes, luck was a lady. He couldn't know that the Buick would make their next decision, breaking down a country short of their destination. Or that his next bit of luck was to be a lady named doña Luz.

Two days later and just over another border, the Buick stalled at a light and wouldn't start.

They had just entered the ragged outskirts of s small city called Las Marias, and were surrounded by juice vendors, billiard parlors, and body shops.

A crowd gathered, children and men. "It's the generator. See the light," said a deep voiced child, looking it at the dashboard.

"Lord, that's what it is," admitted Willi. "I didn't notice it. Is there a shop around?"

"Yes, a shop," said the competent child. He consulted three men eating tortillas on their lunch break, returned, and the four of them pushed; a number of boys and a popsicle vendor on his three wheeled bike followed. There was a mechanic's shop just three blocks ahead, beside a Lux Cola plant.

"Do we have a part in the trunk?" Carl asked. They had brought some extra parts.

"No, damn! no!" Willi said.

Carl, who spoke best, followed the mechanic. The repair would take five days. They could get back to the pensión in town on the blue and silver bus line.

"How much?" Willi asked.

"I didn't ask."

They had started to walk when the mechanic came after them. Another mister, he would take them into town.

"Hi, ya." A thin-faced man in a red and black flannel leaned out the window of an old gray Renault. "Get in." He pulled to the curb, leaned back over the seat and opened the back door with a screw driver. Willi got in front, Carl and Blanche in back.

"My name's Frank Bachelor. You folks from the school?"

"No, we just came."

"Oh, we were expecting a family end of the month. To finish out the term."

"What term are you talking about?"

"Well, Campo Alegre, the American School. So you're not from around here?"

"No, stuck here," Willi said. "The generator went."

"Oh, bad! Where were you going?"

"Salvador."

"Oh hey! We spent the summer near there, in La Riña. That was a great place. I was going to teach radio repair at the trade school; but Rainey, my wife, had to be here for the baby. We have Rh factor. We thought they could take care of it here, changing the blood; but they botched it and the baby died. Most of the American wives go back to Houston, even for normal births. Rainey's upset. We're leaving end of the month."

"What American wives are you talking about?" Carl asked.

"The American companies."

"What American companies?" It had never occurred to him to expect other North Americans here.

"Celanese, Borden, a few at the air force base. They support the school."

"My God!"

"Well, it's just as well. Thing is, we have four kids, and even though I'm earning dollars not pesos, my salary doesn't reach. It's only two thousand five hundred a year. That's O.K. for a single girl comes here for an experience. We made out when Rainey was teaching too; but with maids walking out on us in the middle of breakfast, things like that; and another of them losing Franky, my littlest, in the market ... Rainey had to quit. Then the baby. She's upset, as I said. You can't blame her. But, I don't know, I was damned happy here, especially in La Riña. I really wanted to teach at the Tech. It would have been really *doing* something. The salary was peanuts, but you live cheaper.

"But four kids we got."

"What are you going to do?"

"We're going back. We're going to live with Rainey's parents in Radley, Missouri. I've got a job as T.V. repairman. In the summer I'll start my Master's at the University. We're here on a two-year contract. I hate breaking it, but we depended on us both teaching, so. . . . When is your car ready?"

"Not for five days."

"Hey, that's too bad. You can stay with us if you want. You can even have our house permanent; we had a two-year lease, up next August, and we can't find anyone to sublet . . . It's ours, paid for through August. You want it?"

Willi laughed: "You got a job to go with it?"

"Well, there was a social studies teacher supposed to show up last week and no sign of her."

"We haven't got teaching certificates."

"Native English is about all you need here. When the dysentery hits, or hepatitis, they fill in with school secretaries, Spanish teachers, housewives, anyone."

Downtown Las Marias came to an end at a small brown river bridged by a concrete arch painted yellow and terracotta. The opposite bank was lined by large suburban houses.

"Santa Rita over there," Frank said. Most of the North Americans live there."

On the slopes above were pitched hundreds of zinc roofed shacks. A few large tile-roofed country homes lay off to the south of them. Beyond the waterworks was a lovely green park with breadfruit trees. Frank backed up a steep unpaved road.

"Miguelito only makes it in reverse," he explained.

When he stopped under an umbrella-shaped tree in the flat clearing at the top of the hill, nearly ten infants immediately gathered around the car.

"Wash it Mister?"

"Not today," Frank said. *Lávame* was written in the dust of both car doors.

A row of mud shacks faced on the dusty courtyard formed by the widening of the road. In the center of them was a large, two-storied house, its first floor painted red, the second, yellow. Frank pointed to it: "We live there. Got it cheap. It hadn't been rented in two years. Too far from town. It's why we couldn't sublet. Neighborhood's bad too." The car washing crowd moved with him across the courtyard to the door of the yellow-red house: "Your Missus not here," they told him. "She went out to the store." A large dog bounded out as soon as the door was unlocked, scattered them.

The first floor of the house, built into the hillside, included an open garage, occupied by a *pasteleria*; and a dark subterranean room, empty. Inside the door opened by Frank, a stairway led up to the living quarters above. The infants reconvened in the entryway:

"Can Francisco come out?"

The little boy was already waiting on the landing above. Frank took a basket from a row of pegs at the bottom of the stairs, gave it to him: "Bring us three *Polares* and six French rolls, and get the dog in."

"Can I stay out and play after?" Francisco asked.

"Yes. First say hello to my friends. This is my son Franky. He's Francisco to these friends who are so indispensable to him." They climbed the stair, which spiraled rather grandly to the main floor over the garages. "Rainey doesn't like him to play with these kids. I don't see the harm. Only vice they've taught him so far is to urinate behind trees. I don't know. I think that's a healthy thing, mentally and physically, in this climate." Frank laughed. "We call those kids out there our Press Corps. They wait all day to get a glimpse of us going in or out. God! And if we have a visit...! I don't know what they did with themselves before we moved here."

The door banged below: "Here comes the Missus!" shouted an infant. "She bought bananas at Lino's." "She says they are bananas, but they are *plátanos*!" shouted another. "The Missus don't know what's *plátanos* and what's bananas!" "Hey, Francisco, your mama don't know what's a banana and what's a...."

"Francisco, tell your mama that there's visitors. Two misters!" The shouts drowned out the dog's barking.

Frank's wife slammed the door on the uproar, came up the grand stairway. She was pretty despite her faded freckles, poor posture. Frank took the basket from her, introduced them: "They're from Chicago. How about it! Just came here. Nothing to do with the school."

Rainey, friendly, smiled calmly: "Go on out to the patio with Frank. I'll bring lunch as soon as I feed the kids."

Frank wanted to show them the house. "It's crazy. You'll see."

The stairway emerged into a courtyard, paved in terra cotta tile, whitened by rain spatters. In its center, under a patch of enameled blue sky, was a monumental cube, faced in green and yellow tile, topped by another smaller cube, topped by still another. Built into the lower cube were two glass-fronted cabinets and a small sink. The upmost tier formed a niche with a plaster Stella Maris. "The wedding cake," said Frank. "It's a combination bar and altar. Actually I keep my textbooks in it and Rainey washes the yucca and potatoes in the sink. Three dark bedrooms opened off the court. At the back was a smaller patio, with a poured cement table and benches, a small swimming pool, a patch of fenced-in grass, bordered by roses. "It was the roses made us take the house, and the view."

The back of the house looked over Las Tres Marias. "All that down there is ours too." Frank pointed to a back lot descending in several weed-grown terraces to a wire fence and a pair of out buildings. "We thought we'd do something with it, but never had time. The pool takes a lot of work. We had to caulk it and paint; and it has to be scrubbed out once a week. We all get in there in the buff and slosh the old Clorox around. It's been a great place really."

"Fantastic!" said Willi.

"Italian fellow built it, his villa. Without benefit of architect, as you can see. Sometimes I think we're living in some kind of hallucination!" There was another cement and tile altar in the garden, its niche enshrining a bottle of *Agua Damiana*. "He lives in a penthouse downtown now. Press corps down there drove him out, I guess. They stole his chickens, broke his fences, painted *hideputa* on his walls. Rich bastard, owns sixteen laundries, and he won't let us break our lease. Look, here's another bedroom and another bath, and a changing room big enough for a bedroom, except no window. You're welcome to move in right back here, if you want; or you can have the whole place in a month."

Willi was looking around, grinning and nodding, rubbing his palms on his thighs.

"Francisco!" Frank called to the little boy, who had put the basket of Lux Cola on the concrete table. "Now bring us glasses and lemons and the tequila."

"Fantastic," repeated Willi. "Really fantastic."

"Yeah, isn't it? Rainey loved the garden. We had to take it. It's all there was. We started thinning out the jungle in back, to see what we had. There's a mango tree. Five or six banana trees, pineapples, avocados, chirimoya. Press corps gets most of the fruit if you don't watch out; but Rainey keeps the dog back there now, so we did get some mangos this month.

"We're leaving the dog. You wouldn't mind taking her I hope. Anyway, in two months there should be guavas again. It's a fight, though, not only with the press corps, but with the *animalitos*. One suppertime, we were sitting right here, eating with the Esriols--he's a photographer with "La Republica." Wife came to teach psychology at the University. Anyhow, a brigade of ants, a kind they call *ñocales*, marched away with a whole bush while we were eating dessert: petals, leaves, everything; left the bare stalks. Rainey sprayed everything we had in the house on them; didn't even slow them down."

Frank's two older children, a boy and a girl, came out in their bathing suits. "Hello, here comes the team. You haven't much time before lunch," Frank called. They began a game of volleyball, up to their necks in the water. The smallest boy brought out two bottles and some chunky little glasses. "*Gracias, Francisco*," said Frank. "This is Franky, I guess I told you that; girl over there— big as a horse isn't she—is Janey, and the other is Mike. A lot of family for a schoolteacher, right Francisco? So your Mammy bought bananas. Tell her to fry them. We like them that way, don't we?"

"Shall I get mangos Pappy?"

"Ah, yes. We'll have them with our Cruz Verde." Frank poured out four glasses of Cruz Verde. Carl made a face.

"Drink up, man; we've got a broken-down car and nine hundred dollars between us." said Willi, tossing off his glass.

"Give thanks for no kids," said Frank. "Listen, stay here. I mean it." Willi slapped his thigh again, looked around the garden in disbelief. Frank refilled glasses. The little boy brought him a small basket filled with mangos which his father began cutting up with a penknife, handing the first piece to Carl: "Suck on this; the Cruz Verde will go down like a dream." Rainey brought out a plate of Italian bread, a bowl of mashed eggplant seasoned with oil and garlic.

"This is terrific stuff," Willi said.

"Rainey learned to make it from my mother. Dip the bread in it, like this. My grandfather had a Greek restaurant in Somerville, Massachusetts. He was a great man. Rainey and I went to an island off Paros on our honeymoon; we ended up staying a year in a house we rented for twenty dollars a month. A great year. Only thing in the house that reminded you were in the Twentieth Century was Rainey's equipment she got from the Margaret Sanger clinic. And that failed us. Janey was born in Athens. They kept Rainey in bed for two whole weeks afterwards; it's just custom, a perfectly normal birth. When she got up, she fainted! My Rainey, what a girl! She'd never fainted in her life."

"I remember," said Rainey, "looking out the window at all those red roofs and that strange sky. . . . The next thing I knew I was back in the bed again, flat on my back. A little doctor who could hardly see over the bed was saying, 'Madame must not get up so quickly.'"

Frank laughed. "Rainey's a breeder. Schoolteachers shouldn't marry breeders. It's why I think of going somewhere else . . . some cheaper place to live. I think of my kids going barefoot, learning at home with Rainey. In La Riña you could do it; but, well, she's afraid. She's had too much."

Rainey put a plate of fried bananas and bits of veal on the table. They ate with their fingers, the children taking theirs to eat on the grass. A green parrot with a new, healthy plumage descended from the lemon tree beside the table and climbed to Frank's shoulder, taking the pencil from behind his ear and splitting it with his beak. The bird's circular pupils flashed like semaphores. "Roberto is a fine fellow," Frank said. "He's going back with us. Only thing we're taking. No matter how much it costs in bribes and certificates."

"He'd sooner leave me than Roberto," said Rainey.

"Listen," said Frank, "Stay. How about it? A rent free house."

"We'd pay something," said Willi.

"No, no, I don't want your money. Don't talk about that yet… You like it here, don't you?"

Willi grinned, scratching his head.

"Good," said Frank "We won't talk any more about it just yet. I just wanted to know if you liked it. Think it over, that's all." He got up from the bench, handed Roberto back into the tree. "Hey, we take *siestas*. How about you? It's damn hot at this hour."

"I'll stretch out by the pool if it's all right," Will said.

"Sure, great. I'll give you a suit. You want a bed, chose any one you like."

Carl fell asleep on a cot in the back bedroom. There was a high window opening to the kitchen and a door opening to the patio.

His dreams came and went. Once or twice he woke swimming in perspiration. In one dream, Blanche came in to the room to talk to him the way she had in Chicago after she had quarrels with his cousin John. Though she was engaged to John, whose family lived in the other half of their duplex on Lowell Street, she lay on his bed with her legs apart, telling him how she had spent a summer sleeping in Boston Common while her parents thought she was at a special summer camp for troubled adolescents: expensive but they'd manage... "Put your skirt down," he told her. He woke then and slept again and his mother was in the room. He told her his idea of going with Willi, to the place with the lawns for butterflies and the liquor made from honey and orange peel that made your head buzz, and the mules you could capture and ride up to the top of the mountain.

He woke to wipe his head with the sheet and slept again and Blanche was there:

"Listen, Carl, I didn't know what was real and never would in that nice raised ranch in Laurel Heights." Blanche said and laughed until she cried. A kind of disintegration, her laugh.

Then the short-wave voice of Fidel Castro on Willi's Telefunken: the care of pigs, the tasseling of corn. In perfectly lucid, to him, Spanish...

Juan y Pablo Llevan un fiambre al Parque del Libertador ...

The voices on the Berlitz tape.

"I'm sure that's going to be very useful," said Blanche, starting one of their old stoned conversations. "Shall I go with you? My fiancé is going off to war."

"Sure, come."

It all happened very slowly. A couple sentences could fill an hour. She picked up his things, his books off the bed. "What's this?"

"Fanshen. It's Willi's. Willi's a Maoist."

"Is a Maoist the same as a Marxist?"

"No. A Maoist bases his revolution on the rural masses. Marx based his on the industrial proletariat. That's why we're going to Salvador, because of the rural masses."

"*Que dia mas encantador, dice Clara.*" The Berlitz tape again.

"What's that mean?" Blanche asked, spreading her legs on his bed.

"What an enchanting day."

"Gawd! I mean the world is crazy, Carl, and people can still say things like that?"

"I guess somewhere people still do," he said and woke.

He was shivering. A breeze was blowing in through the open door over his half naked body.

Just outside the little room, the maid, Augustina, was hanging some flapping sheets on a clothesline; and talking to the parrot.

"*...como que te vas a mizuree,* Old Big Beak."

"Aaark! *Mala. En mala hora.*" hallooed the bird, Roberto.

"They could take me. I work. I no sit in a tree and do nothing..."

"Aaark!"

"What you do in Miz ur ee, old Big Beak?" A sheet was snapped angrily. "They take me I make myself better. I work in a factory and rent myself a little room. I buy a fur coat to keep myself warm. I make six dollars the hour. How you think you going to keep yourself warm, eh?
Maldito loro. How you think you keep yourself warm in miz ur ee?"

Tuesday afternoon, Frank drove them to the shop on the Avenida Quinta. The place was crowded with cars and parts. They didn't see the Buick anywhere. A different mechanic was working, looked uncomprehending at the mention of a 1957 Buick.

"Green," Willi said. "It stopped out there." He pointed down the street. "They pushed us here. Saturday." The mechanic went behind a disassembled Toyota and brought forth another mechanic.

"Ah, yes. It's outside." He led them out a back door to the muddy lot behind. There it was. "We have not done anything."

"Why not?" yelled Willi.

"You said to us, if we could get an old part..."

"Yes, yes..."

"There were no old parts. To order new costs five hundred pesos and takes four weeks to deliver. We could not order without speaking to you."

"It doesn't sound right," "Frank said. "Ramos knows where I live. Why didn't he send a message?"

The man shrugged. "Maybe he, did not think you would know... where was the other, the other...*mister.*"

"Where is Ramos?"

"He will be in at noon."

Frank motioned Carl and Will outside: "Listen. I trust Ramos, within reason. He's kept my Renault running, adapted VW parts for it, so it's actually' a better car than it was. But, still, this doesn't sound right; there out to be a Buick, or at least a G.M. generator out there. We've got to wait till noon anyway, so we can check down the street. Most of the junkyards are in this area."

"Maybe a distributor, not a generator,'" said the first dealer. "And not under five thousand; it wouldn't pay me."

"I'm convinced," said Willi. "Let's have a beer and go home. I'll make

Ramos a present of the car."

"Hey, hold it! He'll sell the parts in that car for more than you paid for it. I'd like to check the place myself. It's the only way we'll find out for sure about the part."

They checked three lots. Cars, stripped down and intact, were piled three and four high in the narrow lots. Frank, small boned and agile, crawled into every accessible Buick, Chevy, and Olds. Willi, fearing his weight on the upper levels, checked a few cars at the bottom. Nothing. "O.K." said Frank after two hours of searching, "We'll have that beer now." It was nearing noon.

In front of the Lux Cola factory, they found a kiosk beginning to fill. A dusty wind blew through. "Got a refrigerator here?" Frank asked. "Beer's cold," said the attendant, and it was. They ordered bottled lemonade for their thirst, then two Polares each.

"I'm thinking," said Frank, "You can do two things. You haven't got the thousand, right?"

"Right!"

"Well then you can sell it yourself, for parts. Which might be difficult. You being Gringos and all, ha ha!

"It's, it's less the language than the rosy . . . the rosy cheeks." Frank laughed.

"Ha, ha," said Willi. "Spare the compliments."

"Face it," said Frank. "They'd cheat you. And, well, me, they'd cheat, all of them, except maybe Ramos. So, the practical thing you could do is try to sell it to Ramos. But for a good price, or..."

"Or what?"

"Or sell it to me. That is...I can't buy it outright, but I can pay the thousand Ramos wants—actually, I think he'd take eight-fifty. Then you take the Renault, with all its. beautiful VW accessories, that you have to take up the hill in reverse; and in a couple years, you see, you see if you can make it to Radley, Missouri in it and we'll switch back, with maybe a few financial arrangements to suit Rainey. As for me, I'll take a clear exchange and forget who's beholden.

"Thing is, my kids don't fit in the Renault. They were smaller when we came. Actually, we came on the bus, and I just bought Miguelito to get Rainey and me to school. We squeezed in for weekend trips, but it was damned uncomfortable. Well, we could take the bus again, but Rainey's had a hard time. I'd like to take her home in comfort; and there's Roberto.

"I admit it's a damned rotten car. I don't think anyone's anyone ever made a worse car than that Renault, and once you're across the border nobody'll repair it for you. It will be pure junk you'll have to pay to haul away. But Ramos can set it up for a couple of years dependable running, I really think."

"You got a deal," said Willi.

"Well, Wait, man, you can think it over a day or two. I think we both ought to. I mean first I thought you'd be owing me money, then I got to thinking I'd be owing you. We got to figure it out calmly... take a day or two..."

"No, it's a good idea. You got the money right away?"

"Yeah, I think so."

"Good, let's go order the part."

"*Hombre*, you got me flustered." Frank said. "I don't like to think of you backing up that hill with all the press corps splitting their sides..."

"You talk like no-good business man."

"No, well, I never said I was a good one. It would be great for Rainey. The Buick... And for Roberto. Well, listen. I throw in the house. O.K.? Till September, rent-free. That makes me feel better."

"No-good bargainer. Let me get Ramos down to eight-fifty," Willi said. "I don't trust you for that. I can do it, O.K. I can do it with infinitives! What do you think?"

"I think yes."

"Let's go, then. We to pay eight-fifty. You not to cheat us, Ramos, old *hideputa!*"

"*Hombre*, you are a man to do business with! We do it! You take the house you hear, and the rent thrown in until September. The mangos will ripen again in another month and then in three months the chirimoyas. Wait'll you see the harvest. And I get the Buick, and to take Rainey back in comfort. So, in a year, we'll talk and find out who's beholden, if that's possible, *hombre*, if that's possible..."

So they stayed. Getting jobs wouldn't be easy, Frank warned. For every unskilled job, there were thousands of unemployed natives. They started with the U.S. companies. Willi, who'd spent a summer boning chickens, got a foreman's job at a canning plant. He had to take a native salary, and found most of his time taken up sending daily reports to a Mr. Harris in Portland, Maine about the greasy state of the floors, the lack of paper towels in the men's john. It was being nowhere.

An afternoon, passing a print shop, he saw they still used an old Chandler Price letterpress of the type his father used to have in the cellar to print wedding napkins and business cards.

He knew everything about that press, make-ready, feeding.

"Half a native salary . . ." He offered himself.

But this just embarrassed them.

Besides they didn't need. anyone. Still, he hung around.

"Pay me whatever you can, and I can show you how to make another guidepin out of tin, and your belt there needs dressing."

So they took him. Carl couldn't believe such a subtle end had been attained with the few broad swipes of Spanish Willi possessed.

Carl's Spanish was another matter. He bought a novel every other day in the Libreria Central, starting with the illustrated *Fotonovelas* with their speech balloons, and progressing to poets, Vallejo, Páez, Rubén Darío—reading at the cement table on the patio afternoons. Mornings he inquired about jobs without success. He hadn't any skills to offer the American companies, and they were suspicious of him—what was he doing here? It left the school, which held out a promise of something temporary later.

"Feels like a subway," Blanche said, waking a morning before six. "Is there a subway here?" She giggled.

"Earthquake!" yelled Frank in the front bedroom. "Earthquake, all out!" He was standing in the center of the patio, as children carrying blankets and pillows went by, waving his arms, directing traffic. "Out in the street. Out in the street. This is a heavy tile roof, and if it comes down..."

There was another tremor. Dishes fell out of the dining room cupboard. It sounded like a train passing. "Hurry up now. Hurry up now," Frank yelled good-humoredly. Augustina, who'd already been up, grinding the corn *masa*, cowered in the doorway of. the kitchen: "*Ave Maria, ave Maria purisima!*" A pot fell onto the stove; some tiles fell out of the altar.

"Out!" Frank yelled at her. "Out!" She wouldn't move. Willi took her by the hand and pulled her down the stairs. In the street below, the press corps was whooping about. A sign had fallen off the *panaderia* on the corner. The inhabitants of the house next door were in the street in their nightclothes. "*Ave Maria, ave Maria purisima,*" Augustina crossed herself and knelt in the red dust. Another tremor, rumbled up from the waterworks. Then it was over.

"Wow!" Willi said. Frank examined the walls. There was a vertical fault in the brickwork, visible where the stucco had fallen off, as if the right side of the facade had sunk slightly. "Get out the old plaster bucket," Frank said.

"You just cover it up?" asked Willi.

"What else. The structure's sound. Guadua poles hold up the roof. They flex, and the wood floor too. The plaster is just frosting on the cake."

They went back in, Rainey carrying little Mike, who was crying. Augustina swept up the fallen plaster, some broken dishes. Frank got out a bucket of grout and started sticking back the tiles fallen from the altar. "Fix it right away," Frank said. "Prevents the earthquake neurosis. You can't let them unnerve you."

Rainey brought coffee, scrambled eggs. They ate in the open, on the back patio. The children walked about with their pillows and blankets in their arms. Little Franky was asleep on the concrete bench.

The days passed. The mangos ripened.

Blanche lay under the mosquito net smoking some stuff Willi bought from an old man at the Cafe de a Media Luna on Calle Septima.

"I'm blue. I can't get high on this stuff."

"Stop then." Carl told her

"I'm blue and I'm hot."

"Think about something else."

"When I'm hot I like to think about being hot."

"All right then think about it."

"Hot, hot, hot!" She flopped over on her side. "Do you like me, Carl?"

Carl put down his *fotonovela*. "I like you."

"Better than Linda Escobar?". Frank had gotten him a little job now, tutoring Linda's little boy who went to the American school. He was delicate after recovering from meningitis and studying at home for the time...

"She interests me. I don't want to sleep with her."

"What interests you?"

"She worries about such funny things, and she's unhappy in her position. I admire her for that."   Linda couldn't get used to many things here, with what she considered her falsely exalted position being the wife of a factory manager, having to deal with maids etcetera.

"I'm unhappy in my position."

"I know."

"But. I'm not interesting."

"You're not like her. You're free to change."

"What do you mean?"

"You could go back"

"Do you want me to?"

"No. I love you."

He worried about her. She didn't fit any of the categories of Las Marias women. North American women had husbands and children and houses in Santa Rita; women of the lowest class worked or were mistresses and whores. She supported idleness well. At the beginning, she tried helping Augustina with the cooking, but didn't know what to do with the unfamiliar foods that the girl brought from the *galeria central*. So Augustina continued to cook for them out of a notebook full of recipes Rainey had translated from *The Joy of Cooking*. "*Pollo a la Tocineta*," she would inform them belligerently, plopping down the dish. It reappeared every Monday. Tuesday was *Higado en su nido de papas*," and so on. Augustina, who also washed the clothes in the stone tub at the back, and swabbed the floors, didn't need any instruction in what foreigners liked.

A few of Rainey's acquaintances had tried to be friendly to Blanche, but she didn't seem formed for intimacy with other women.

Willi worked mornings on the terrace, behind the laundry tubs, every morning the same overcoming, the same plunge into work; it was like athletics, you couldn't be flat-footed. He was painting in goache on fiberboard. Blanche posed for him on a tumbled cot where she afterward took her nap, or sitting at the cement table with a rum bottle in front of her, or stretched out under the plantains. He loved the plantains; he'd never painted anything as satisfying as a plantain leaf.

He drew her drowsing on pillows or sitting at the cement table eating an orange. One day she sat on the parapet watching the press corps in the dusty street below. A scruffy man had come along the road from Aguascalientes and sat on a boulder to rest. The press corps pressed around this new interest which became even more interesting when the man took some coins out of his pocket and laid them on the rock.

"*Ves, que tiene plata.*"

Suddenly he threw the coins, over their heads, across the dusty courtyard. They ran, yelling, to recover them, pushing aside the smaller ones, causing them to scrape their knees. Two boys fought. She watched drowsily thinking, it's spring at home. I'm missing the spring . . . Her father, Harry, was locked away for chronic alcoholism. She thought she'd write Harry in his institution. Maybe he'd know where Belle was, her mother.

Again the man threw, this time behind him, down the slope. Again they ran; again, the little ones got nothing; returned, weeping to the man's lap: "*Bobos, tienen que correr,*" he scolded them, pushing them off, trying to make them run. There was another fight, and the loser limped off home. She noted how the cameo blooms, which had come out just the day before, were lying now, ankle deep in the street. Yes, she thought, I'll write Harry.

"It's springtime here too," Carl had said last night when she'd noted the fact of missing it. *Primavera*, it was called. But what was *primavera*? Just some weather the winds brought over the *cordillera*. It was wet; that was *invierno*, or it was dry, the mountains burned, the cameo bloomed; nothing to do with spring, with seedlings in the window, with that tremendous cranking over the whole tremendous machinery that made the sun go down hours later or earlier. Here the sun set every day at six.

She would write Harry.

Again the man threw. Half of the children were in tears, the other half crowing over their mounting stores of *centavos*. Why does he do it? She felt depressed. The man was evil. His money was evil. Where there was hardship he was spreading misery. She scratched a mosquito bite thinking, yes she would write. At least you always knew where Harry was. Last she'd known of Belle she was in St. Louis married to a man who owned a salon for treating baldness; but that marriage, she knew from Harry, was over in 1962. Belle had moved alone to somewhere in the East.

Again the man threw. "*Corran babosos*," he called turning his pockets out. He would have done better buying himself a pair of shoes, she thought noting his flapping soles.

The hair salon husband, unlike poor Harry, had been rich. Maybe Belle had something from him, could spare her something. She'd feel better if she had a bit of money her own.

"*Los grandes quedan con todo!*" wailed a child, throwing herself on the grass under where Blanche sat. Poor child, she thought. What if she were to drop her a coin? But no! It would only make things worse. Such a pretty little girl, with fine features, a fat little belly glimpsed through her torn dress, nice sturdy little legs though covered with dust. I would love a child, she thought. I would adopt one of these if Carl won't let me have one. Then I would be happy. It's what I need to make me happy.

After Willi was finished, she fell asleep in the chaise. Willi, pleased with his morning's work, sweated over his lunch. He shared Augustina's mess of rice and beans, then had a cigar and a short nap before going to the print shop.

"*No sirve!*" said Zamora. The ink was wrong for the coated paper they were using. Cutting it with linseed oil blurred the photo engraving. "*No importa*, no importa." It was only a political poster; but Willi wasn't happy, found some dusty cans of ink in the store room. They wasted an hour; the cans had no labels. Willi sorted them after a fashion. "*No importa*," Zamora reiterated. He found one that served, but it was green. They ran it; Hugo, still faster than Willi, put through three hundred in two hours. Willi took over, ran two hundred. They'd get it done by next afternoon: "*Bueno, bueno*." They cleaned off plate and rollers, covered the wells with a sheet of plastic. He hated clean up, a job his father used to leave to him. It would be more efficient to run shifts till they were finished, but Zamora liked to close up, roll down the iron grille.

"Pretty, the green," said Zamora, hanging one up: PROGRESO &

EMPLEQ, Ruiz Nogales. Shifty green face. The floor was spread with them. They left and stopped for a Cruz Verde in the cantina at the corner. Zamora talked about the new offset presses. Trouble was the Chandler Price still paid.

"You ever want to sell it, I'll buy it," Willi said.

"What would you do with it?"

"Wood engravings, like the old days."

"No call for it," Zamora said.

Every day was the same as the one before. That was what Willi liked. Only Blanche's poses changed, and his thinking about his line.

A slow line, Willi thought. Thoughtful, hesitant line, dividing Blanche substance from concrete substance, leaf substance. Slow, see what slow can do. Overcome facility. Picasso, overcoming facility all his life. Slow, slow; this side, bush, this side, girl. He held the crayon in his left hand.

"Why do you look at me like that?" Blanche asked.

His uninstructed left hand. When it gains too much art, he'll hold it in his toes. No shadow, no mass, just this line . . . "Can you hold it just another minute." She had a wonderful shape, long necked, long waisted. The shredded banana leaves lifted in the breeze with a leathery sound. The press corps were in the subterranean garage again, shrieking with laughter.

"You like me, Willi?"

"Sure."

"I mean in a certain way."

"I don't like complications."

"There wouldn't have to be." She hadn't had a period for two months. But that was because of the change of water, she thought.

Between the two of us we can't make her happy, Willi was thinking.

"Carl never gets back till three."

"I'll take you to the Tertulia for a Cruz Verde."

"All right." She jumped up and put on her skirt.

The Tertulia roared with talk. They took an inside table as the sidewalk tables were filled. Willi was happy. His work that morning felt like victory. Blanche caused stares when she walked in; women didn't come here. Clodo Gomez, whom Will knew from the neighborhood, came and sat with them, bringing his racing paper and spreading it on the table.

"Let me initiate the little Miss. You will see; betting is divine when you put your mind to it. But only the favorites at the start. Start out with the favorites. One must have a system." "A system, yes," said a man reading at the next table. The Tertulia lent out cheap paperback books: collections of poetry, manuals on hypnotism and sexual techniques, *fotonovelas*.

Pepe Joroba came in. Pepe Joroba was forty-two years old and had written eighty-three plays. Willi had met him at a party at the print shop, when one of his plays, which they printed for him, came out. Clodo ordered another round of Polares. "Sit down, sit down."

The helicopters were still overhead, but people hardly noticed in this the third week of the counting of election results.

WE REPEAT, WE REPEAT, CITIZENS HAVE NOTHING TO FEAR FROM THE PROTECTORS OF THE FATHERLAND...

"Someone should write a play about this election," Willi said.

"I think I have," said Pepe Joroba. "I wrote a play set in the courtyard of this family works for the electric company. They're all gathered around drinking, listening to the radio night after night, waiting for the election results; because, you see, if the other party gets in the father will lose his job . . . not set here, of course; here we have the glorious Civil Service .

"Byzantium itself," said Clodo.

"You' re right. But back in '53 everyone was a political appointee. It was worse."

"Shall I put Senador or Miel de Abeja for the second choice?" asked Blanche.

"One's as bad as the other. Put Mi Colonel."

"Teachers were the ones made all the trouble. The Intellectual Proletariat." said Pepe.

"There's nothing for it but to put the top favorite in the third. The fourth you can play around a little. There's Bizcocho and Cruz Verde."

"The Intellectual Proletariat," went on Pepe. "Thin soup that lot. Nothing but chalk dust in their pockets, even today." He ordered another round of Polar Beer.

"What do you say? Gemelo or Papel Sellado in the fifth?" asked Clodo.

"Gemelo," Willi said. He didn't know anything about horse racing, but he liked the name.

"That's the favorite," said Clodo. "Gives you four favorites. That's too many. I never put more than three. You put more you divide the pot with fifty thousand other *miserables*."

"Let me choose," Blanche said. He passed her the form: "Bicho looks good."

"Bicho it is. The ladies have a gift. I ever tell you I win the *Cinco y Seis* twice? The first time I got so excited I got married and made five children before I came to my senses. Second, I would have won, I should say, but I forgot to file the form, and with only three favorites. I considered shooting myself. Nothing is worse than regret. Don't let anyone tell you otherwise. Ah, well, one lives in hope," said Clodo.

A cavalcade of army trucks passed, their tarps flapping.

"Yes, one lives in hope. With the lottery, I have a method. I play the end numbers, regular, each week. That way you are bound to win, one or two hundred pesos a month. The money I win I play on the whole number. One lives in hope, yes! *jugar es divino!*"

CITIZENS SHOULD MAINTAIN CALM...

The voice was overhead again. "Good Lord," Willi said. "I thought it was over."

"It takes at least another week," said Clodo.

THE AIR FORCES WISH TO ASSURE CITIZENS OF THEIR NEUTRALITY.

"I want another *Cinco y Seis,*" Blanche said.

"Allow me," said Clodo Gomez, and, taking a ten peso bill from his wallet, he sent the shoeshine boy to the corner tobacco store. Blanche tried to pay him but he waved her off.

PEOPLE SHOULD REMAIN IN THEIR HOUSES AWAITING THE RESULTS...

"Remain in our houses indeed!"

"Yes, this play. I had two endings," said Pepe. "I could never decide if I wanted it to end well or bad. One of them was they win...their party wins. The hero will keep his job, so they have this wild final party with fireworks and radios blaring. All on stage. I remember something like it really happened in my neighborhood. Only it was a water commissioner's assistant...lived back of me, kept me awake night after night, *en visperas.*

"The other ending was tragic. Twelve kids and no job. I don't remember which I decided on. I have a difficult time knowing if my muse is tragic or comic."

Willi bought a round, and Blanche filled out another card with no favorites, and they walked back, past the *por puesto* drivers, waiting on the Avenida Sexta for four fares so they could head out full for Rionegro; through the waterworks, and up the long hill home. "I'm going to play the horses every week," Blanche said. Belle would like the idea. She tapped the acacia leaves overhead into tiny fists. The city smelled of black beans, a thousand evening meals cooking.

She hadn't had a period for twelve weeks now. Only this funny brown spotting. There was something wrong with her. Maybe it was cancer.

Blanche, Carl thought, desirable Blanche, who'd come to his childhood bed and given herself to him on this same bed, among his books and model airplanes. He felt her unhappiness.

If they'd been at home would she have long since moved on, hitchhiked on across the country? Here, to behave in her old free and easy way, was unthinkable. Here, they lived in the house of a laundry tycoon. He read Linda Escobar's handsome editions from Spain and Argentina. They were vaguely upper class, if they could be classified at all. The upper classes, here, didn't drop out and employ themselves as gardeners and bricklayers.

"Maybe she should have a child," Willi said. "A child would amuse her."

"What do you think?" Carl asked him.

"I don't think much of the idea, frankly. A child isn't a pet."

"True."

"Do you mean personally . . . a child of mine, or any, any child?" Willi asked.

"Both."

"Well, personally, I consider I'm the end of my family. I've always felt that. I. was the only one. No sisters and brothers, no first cousins either side, my mother over forty when I was born. An exhausted line. Families die. I've always looked on myself that way, an end . . . the one to express it all maybe, all the armchairs and china cupboards and pot roasts and cabbage soups . . . press it all into some kind of shape and make an end...

"And as to *any* child; well, we're an exhausted empire is my opinion, the end of a line. One or two more generations, what do they mean? Better to use the opportunity to protest, make a statement."

Carl always asked her if she had her diaphragm in, and usually she did, only now and then, about one night in ten, say, she left it out and lied to him. It was like a recurring need with her, deceiving people. It made life flavorful; taking a chance like this was like playing the lottery. Besides it wasn't much of a risk, she'd thought; she was probably sterile, her mother had a friend who was sterile because of her periods.

Her last period was somewhere back before they crossed the last border. Blanche tried to remember exactly when, but couldn't. There was only this little brown spotting and one morning a brisk flow into the john, and then nothing. It just stopped.

Then, a Sunday morning she woke with her nightgown soaked, bad cramps.

Willi had medical coverage through his job at the printers, so he posed as husband, and called the *Seguros*. A doctor came, said it looked like a miscarriage and sent her to the Clínica Carvajal.

"But weren't you careful?" Willi asked Carl.

"Of course. She has a diaphragm."

They scraped her out and she slept all Friday. When she woke, she found herself in a long ward between a woman with a large smooth baby and a woman with a small wrinkled one. The family of the woman with the large baby camped all around her, eating out of stackable aluminum pans.

Next day, she felt better, and got up to get a closer look at the babies. I had a baby in me all that time, this astonishing thing happened to me and I never once believed in it, she thought. Willi came and held her hand. Carl went out to buy her a raspberry ice.

She tried to ask one of the nursing sisters what the fetus had been.

Un muchachito, she was told, *de cuatro meses*. She had ben four months pregnant, and all the time she thought she was sterile.

Well, it didn't matter. Probably she'd never be able to carry a baby more than four months. Belle had known a woman like that.

They threw a party a week before Frank and Rainey left. Japanese lanterns were strung around the pool. Rainey set all her Greek dips out on the concrete table and Frank and Augustina roasted a goat in the barbeque pit. Mostly it was people from the school who came, along with some Peace Corps people and a couple of teachers from the university.

Carl sat at the edge of the pool with his feet in the water while Blanche swam lazily back and forth, listening to a group of Rainey's friends who had gathered round her:

"...and supermarkets! Not to have to bargain over every squash and grapefruit...that will be a relief..."

"...and not to bring the black berries home wrapped in a banana leaf..."

"I'll probably buy everything I see, at least once," said Rainey.

"And have a washing machine instead of a washerwoman. Your clothes won't miss being slapped on stones. And you won't miss your washerwoman squatting in the middle of the patio and lighting candles to keep off devils..."

Heard from the wives. And then, from a group of Peace Corps workers:

"Myth...in the mountain villages a headless horseman is said to be seen at the equinox..."

"...persistent myth in all of it of course. And then there's the worldwide influence of Catholicism..."

Frank led someone up to him at that point, and Carl stood to shake hands with an older gentleman wearing a suit and tie:

"Rafael Villegas," Frank said. "His nephew is in my history class."

"*Encantado*, yes," said Sr. Villegas. "It is a shame, I admit, that I send my sister's child to your school. He will go to MIT, I hope, and study mining, as I did, and spend his life most likely in a place like Colorado, thus depriving this benighted country further of its professional class; but one must think of the child, yes…"

Carl moved with Sr Villegas over to the back wall of the patio. "MIT is a very good school."

"Yes," said Sr Villegas. "And there is the Colorado School of Mines. That is my Alma Mater. The Mother of my soul, ha, ha! I was unfortunately brought up to believe these mountains were the Mothers of my Soul…" Sr. Villegas waved his hands off to the north where the *cordillera* glowed lavender in the sunset. "Are you familiar with the Colorado School of Mines?"

"Well, no. I went to a very small church college. It was founded by my ancestors, so I was given a scholarship. I studied literature, things like that."

"Ah, literature." Sr Villegas put his punch glass down on the parapet with an elegant gesture and accepted a crust spread with *baba ganoush* from Rainey. "My wife is a lover of literature. She reads English. She longs to speak English well. You must meet her."

He gave Carl his card. He was president of Cementos Valle. Perhaps it could be parlayed into a job, he thought, putting it carefully into his shirt pocket.

There were aftershocks for a few weeks. The mountains burned, the soot settling on the white tablecloth of the patio table. The chirimoyas ripened. Augustina taught Blanche to cook rice and to soap their clothes in the cement tub and lay them on the grass in the noonday sun to bleach. When Willi got a little raise, they decided they could keep her on for two days a week, after Frank left. She could keep her room and work for the neighbors the other five days.

Don Rafa was pleased to hear from Carl. His offices were not in the plant but downtown on the Avenida Lugo. Carl must pay him a call.

He went on foot on Monday morning and found the office on the third floor of the Edificio Zacour, which stood up painfully between two bulldozed remains of neighboring buildings that had never been rebuilt following an earthquake in '61. There was a tank at the corner, and a soldier posted in the doorway. The presidential votes were still being counted.

"So, you are a young man who loves literature." *Don* Rafa got up from behind his desk and came around to shake Carl's hand. "I always go at this hour to the café downstairs. You will come?"

The Café Candelaria roared like the surf. The doors to the street were all open, and from a helicopter overhead a voice was broadcast counseling calm:

"Calm!" cried *don* Rafa raising a fist.

"A cretin calm. The people is in love with calm. Even the young men. When I think of myself at twenty, at twenty-four, sitting up all night among journalists and desperate men plotting assassinations... You, what do you think of such calm?"

"Well, I'm not too interested in politics," Carl said. "Are things really very dangerous?"

"No, it is merely, if there is a change of government, some workers for the state electric, and so forth, lose their jobs to people of the opposing party. It is simple self-interest. And of course the count takes nearly a month, so during that time everyone sits up all night to worry and dispute. So, you are not interested in politics. What is your interest then? What did you expect to find in this cursed place?"

"I don't know...some space, some..." He thought of the afternoons he spent with Willi in the dark bar on Canning Street, Willi nursing bottles of ale and a growing grudge against the country his German Socialist father had chosen to emigrate to in the Forties. Like this café, there were newspapers spread across the tables, and loud talk at the bar. Here it was louder, like the surf.

"Explain it to me. I don't understand." Don Rafa made a gesture toward a waiter, who came and took an order for *café tinto* and *aguardiente* with a dish of limes.

"Well, my friend Willi is looking for what he might call 'real'...real work...I can't explain it very well. And of course he wanted to paint."

"And you?"

He wanted to say that perhaps he was looking for beauty, for goodness... but it was a much too embarrassing thing to say. He had read a good bit of Tolstoy in the past year, and thought of himself as a type of Levin.

THE PEOPLE MUST AWAIT IN CALM...

The voice from the sky caused the roar to cease.

"Ah, yes! We are to wait calmly with tanks in the streets." jeered don Rafa. "Yes, you were saying..."

"Just some space..." Carl struggled with his thought. "Some clarity...to begin my life."

"Some clarity! Ah, dark, dark it would have to be for someone to come here looking for light!" cried don Rafa. "Aye, I'm an old man..."

THE RESULTS OF TODAY'S ELECTION, WHICH WILL BE...

"Not so old I don't remember, no. Once I read poetry. When we were not plotting assassinations we read poets and walked into the streets at dawn, haggard and ecstatic, yes! But then he died in his bed…"

"Who was that?" asked Carl.

"The villain we planned to assassinate…!"

THERE WILL BE NO MILITARY COUP…

"Twelve years we talked… Aye, perhaps you are right in not caring for politics. I had a cousin once, became very rich. He used to say to me, 'What is this running with journalists and going to jail?' 'I love this accursed country,' I said. 'I want to save it.'

"To save it, Oh God! I was twenty-three.

"It doesn't do, perhaps," he went on, waving again for the waiter, "It doesn't do to love an entire people…"

WE REPEAT, NO MILITARY COUP…

"*Aye, caray*, these elections. Six weeks to count the ballots. What kind of a country is this? The devil's own. But what was I saying? Ah yes, 'One must learn to love what one possesses,' my cousin told me, 'A wife, a son….' He has five sons. I have none. But his meaning is the same: To love one's own life and want to begin it, as you do." The waiter came with the order. The volume of talk surged to overcome the drone of the helicopter each time it passed overhead.

"He became very rich, this cousin of mine. He put all his sons through university abroad. The last son, I remember, told his father he wished to study law at the Universidad Nacional, that this was a good starting-out point for any career. Well, to this my cousin replied, 'The best starting.' out point, *mi hijo*, the best starting out point is aboard an international flight at Chiapitas International Airport!' How about that, eh?" *Don* Rafa clapped Carl on the shoulder and downed his *café tinto* in one gulp..

THE GOVERNMENT COUNSELS CALM and patience…

The helicopter was moving off .to another part of the city.

"Ah yes, calm, calm and patience when it takes a month and a half, the counting! In your country they have the voting machine even in the smallest village. No need to wait with tanks in the streets. No wonder there are plots. So, you are a teacher of English."

"No, no. I just thought your wife would desire some conversation…we might read things and talk about them after."

"Mrs. MacWhirter tells me you are a fine teacher." The fact that don Rafa knew Linda MacWhirter was Carl's first indication of how interwoven was the life of the city.

"She is too kind, but I might help someone, I suppose, to learn English."

"My wife has all her afternoons free. You will come on Friday to make arrangements, yes."

"Yes, yes, I'll be happy to."

"She is an idle woman like them all, but intelligent. She amuses herself with languages. We shall see. I'm quite sure you will serve."

Don Rafa lived in el Barrio Santa Rita and always walked home at nightfall. Carl walked with him up the Calle Quinta, as it was his way home too, and they cut through the water works, climbing the path that circled the treatment plant, and pausing at the top of the hill to look down on Las Marias.

"Used to come up here and fly huge muslin kites shaped like buzzards when I was a boy. When they'd break loose they'd fall into the palms of the Plaza Central... Ah, yes. Just look at all those lights, not a flicker." The sun had just sunk behind the Cordillera Oriental and the lights of San Fernando were winking on. "'If you didn't know it was Las Marias you might think it was Paris,' as my old friend Feliciano Bustamante used to say, and we'd remember how twenty years ago they hadn't the hydroelectric and all that side was dark.

"Ah, yes. It was Feliciano and I put the power plant in, in 1942, it was. 'Is that San Roque over there?' he'd say.

"'That it is,' I'd say. Used to be the Jesuit seminary was as far as San Roque went. My wife, Lucita wanted to buy a lot out there in 1950. If I'd bought two or three...be a millionaire today...

"She has a good head for a woman, I have to admit. But then, it could have happened the city spread to the east...God, to think that thirty years ago they had no electric power there's that fellow in Chocó sending up a satellite. Truth. It was in the newspaper. He's made a launching pad of bamboo. Lucita read it. Not going to be able to send it up, though. There's a bunch of women's organizations objecting to the monkey..."

"Monkey...?"

"They wanted to send up a monkey, the poor wretch, but the women's organizations have the monkey *incomunicado* in Los Olmos, and a court order to have the poor fellow undergo a psychiatric examination, hah! hah! It's what happens to the scientific impulse here. Well, you go that way, I go this. Until Friday then."

The following Friday, Carl followed don Rafa's directions to the opposite side of the city. Some large new buildings set well back from the street behind gates housed the Canadian and the Spanish consulates. The Villegas house and some other older houses were halfway up the hill and flush with the street. Backing Miguelito up this hill was a bit more embarrassing than negotiating the hill at home.

An elderly woman opened the door for him. She was not, as Carl thought, a maid, but don Rafa's sister. He was led back through a series of rooms to a dark study where doña Luz sat behind a large table. She stood and stretched out both arms to approach him, laying them on his arms to show a certain warmth, but also, he thought, to fend off the habitual double kiss of greeting.

She was a tall fragile woman and, but for a certain haggardness around her eyes, looked to be much younger than her husband.

"I must show you around, the garden..." She spoke and moved a little awkwardly, probably being unused to using English; but opening the doors to the deep garden behind the study and walking onto its paths seemed to restore her to naturalness. They were two people who would not normally meet, he thought, and she was seeking to smooth the way by showing him something she obviously loved.

"My camellias," she said, plucking off dead blossoms here and there from the rectangular beds and cupping them in her large bony hand. They were an extraordinarily deep coral and at the height of their blooming.

"Lovely," Carl said.

"Are they not? It is fine summer for them."

"Summer...?"

"Well, we call the dry season the summer. Winter is when it rains in February and again in October."

"Ah."

Her hand was full of the crumpled blossoms and she laid them on a cement bench. "*Flores marchitas*," she said. "How is it said in English?"

"Withered flowers. It's nicer in Spanish."

She became uneasy under his gaze. "But let us go back. You must see also the library."

They returned to the dark study and when his vision recovered from the intense light of the garden he saw that three walls were lined floor to ceiling with books. They seemed to be in several languages, mostly French. "You must take any book you wish," she said.

"You are very kind."

"Look them over, perhaps you will see something."

There were translations of English authors: Dickens, Thackeray, Fielding, bound in red leather; unbound French classics printed on creamy paper. He noticed Henry Adams' *Mont Saint-Michel and Chartres*, and took this out.

"You must borrow it, "she said.

"I've read it."

"Oh, then perhaps something else."

"No, no, I meant it's one of my favorite books..."

"Ah, so. A friend gave it to me. We saw the cathedrals together. I read some of it. It is difficult."

"We might read it together."

"Yes, yes, I should like it. We can study right here in this room." She drew shut another blind that was allowing a tiny patch of sun on the rug, and turned on a floor lamp.

"You speak English very well," he said.

"Ah, no. I learn only a little with Mrs. Galloway the doctor's wife. She has gone back to Tennessee with her family; so I look for you…"

"Next week, this same day at three thirty I am free," he said.

"That is good."

"I've never taught before."

"But Mrs. McWhirter speaks very well of you."

"She is too kind. You are too kind."

"You will come next week then." She walked him to through an airy dining room to the door. "And you must take the book." He still had the Henry Adams in his hand.

"Tell me," he said. "Have you seen Chartres?"

"Oh, yes, and you?"

"Never."

"You must, some day."

He thought of his new relationship to his country and the improbability of ever traveling anywhere.

"Yes, yes, but tell me," he said, "did you see it first or read the book first?"

"I saw the cathedrals first." She picked some blown peonies out of a bunch on a table beside the door, held them in her hands as she had held the camellias.

"Then you must go back," he said.

"Ah, no…"

"Couldn't you?" He thought of her as rich, free to do as she wished. "No," she said quite finally. "I marry; I come here. This is my life."

"But you have never wished to go again?"

"No," she said. "I have never wished to change what has been." She smiled and gave him her hand. "Until next week, then."

"Yes, yes," he carried off the book.

Rereading the Henry Adams mornings on the patio was a new pleasure. The book was bound in leather and had thick creamy pages that, after page 160, had to be opened with his penknife. And no one was going to ask him to write a sophomoric paper on it or ask his callow opinion. He would reread all his college books, he resolved. Here under a woodrose vine. And discuss them in a leisurely, adult way with this woman who had left him with an initial impression of her long, stooped body, her intelligent eyes, and her bony cupped hands holding the fading blossoms, *Flores marchitas.*

At the end of June the family left in the Buick, the roof piled high with luggage, and with Roberto in his cage. As the car bumped down the hill, the three of them and Augustina leaned over the parapet to wave goodbye.

"They might have taken me," she wailed.

II

Las Brumas

The fire must have started under the house. The wood floor burned through into the room Willi used for a studio. It was on the opposite end from the bedrooms, so they weren't alarmed until the whole side was in flames, and Elsie the dog barking wildly. Willi saved his short wave, a few of his paintings; and Augustina, her trunk. Blanche and Carl saved their clothes and Carl's books. Engines were summoned, and they stood out in the courtyard in front. The Press Corps danced wildly about, and watched it, all but the walls and grand staircase, burn. Miguelito had been parked across the street, so was saved.

Toward dawn they drove to the *Pensión* Stein on the Avenida Sexta and slept, the three of them, in one room, without washing their bodies or changing their smoky clothes; they didn't wake until three in the afternoon.

Willi was up first. Carl stirred.

"We can't stay here long you know," Willi said.

"No, no!" Carl sat up.

"All we need in one of those mud huts," Willi said. "We might build it ourselves."

Carl got dressed. "I'll talk to The *Doña*."

"Of course, you must come to us at Tula," she told Carl, after he told her about the fire and Willi's idea of the mud hut. She sent him out to find *don* Rafa at the café.

Don Rafa was in his usual place at the Cafe Mil y Una Noches drinking *café tinto*. Carl told him about the fire.

"How?"

"The press corps. I suspect. That's what we call the street kids who hang around us. They smoked in the *bodega*."

"You are all safe?"

"Yes, yes"

"Thank God! But the whole…"

"The whole grand pile. Left the granite staircase and a couple of walls."

"*Cielos!*"

"We need something. A shack. It must be cheap."

"Cheap, yes. A mud shack you mean?"

"Yes. And a little land maybe."

"Mud shacks are in continual need of being shored up. That is if they don't wash away entirely in the rainy season, and *animalitos* infest the thatch aside from numerous other…"

"Your wife suggested Tula."

"Ah, you want to be farmers!"

"Willi would like it." He thought of all the agricultural advice from Fidel

Castro that Willi had taken in over the short wave.

"You will live like peasants."

"We are peasants." Willi, being a Maoist, loved peasants.

"Ah, well now, there is a concrete block hut with a good zinc roof at Las Brumas...

"It has never been much of a farm, belongs to my wife's family actually. I would have made it pay, but they never cared. There are two outbuildings, and one is empty. There was a caretaker, don Luciano, occupied it with his son. The son married and we built another for him. Then don Luciano moved up the hill to Los Franceses. The son does his work. There is little enough since we hardly go now. There was the accident. I fear Luciano blames himself. In any case, the hut is empty. Plenty of land, plantains, bananas, some chickens, one cow. There used to be horses. We used to go all the long vacation with the children, the nephews. Then there was the accident. One of my brother's children was thrown from Luciano's mule. It was a sad occasion. My wife took it the hardest, had the mule and horses sold. We've turned to gardening. Perhaps this year we shall go again. But the hut you are welcome to."

"We would work." Carl insisted.

"But there is Orlando, and his woman helps in the kitchen."

"What is growing there now?"

"Margueritas, bougainvillea."

"To eat, I mean," said Carl

"Well, there are chickens, milk."

"Listen, we'll take it," Carl was excited. "But we must work."

"Work, then, *pues*, work," don Rafa smiled.

"Concrete block hut, zinc roof, plenty of land, in the central *cordillera*..." Carl reported back. Blanche was still in bed, drinking iced coffee.

"We'll go!" Willi said.

They gave Elvis the dog to Augustina, and the Renault to Ramos to sell for them; it would never make it over the *cordillera*. The Laundry Magnate who owned the house made a few feeble gestures at blaming them for the fire, but gave it up in the face of their poverty and the testimony of the baker next door that the urchins continually smoked under the house.

At the Casa del Pueblo they outfitted themselves as cheaply as possible; and the following Thursday they took a bus to the city to catch a *por puesto* taxi to Tuxpan in the state of Tula.

They left before noon, the taxi soaring along the aerial ribbon that crossed the city, leaving to its own slow pace the fussy old town below, its cafes and verandahs behind bougainvillea vines. Autopista del Este, Autopista del Valle; then, looping westward, onto an older mountain road, and they climbed into the clouds hanging over the city.

A bank of clouds sat on the blue eucalyptus tree tops. A shower hung over the far valley.

It was late afternoon when the clouds lifted and they overlooked the city of Tuxpan. A small metal cross with a hubcap hanging on it marked the spot where a car had gone over the cliff. Then they descended through some small villages of white washed houses with heavy black thatch. A square with a church. Grass bleached colorless.

Only the irrigated cane fields were green here. The surrounding hills were burning, the smoke adding to the heat and dust. A woman in front seat got out with her string bags. The final stop was Tuxpan, a taxi stand in front of the cathedral. They unloaded their duffel bags from the roof. It was near dusk; and since there was no electricity at Las Brumas and don Rafa advised not arriving at night, they went across the street and reserved two rooms at a dim little hotel with tall spindly wooden pillars holding up an arcade around a patio full of rubber plants.

Tuxpan was a town of three streets of commerce intersected by two broad boulevards. They walked along one of these boulevards, and found a Chinese restaurant; Chinese restaurants here were identical to Chinese restaurants in Chicago, or presumably anywhere. This one was consoling in their homeless state. Will took out the account book and wrote figures on a napkin: They had about ten thousand pesos saved. "It's my opinion," Willi said, "we should spend only on items like clothes, dentists and food we can't grow, like meat, or we could give up meat. There will be eggs and milk.

"We can grow beans, yucca, tomatoes. We'll each have our jobs: cooking, washing up, washing clothes, plus the cows…"

"Cow," Carl said.

"Yes, and the chickens."

"Have you ever had dealings with chickens?"

"Never. We'll learn. You know," Willi said, "People live here for eight pesos a day. The price of a Coke in a hotel."

"Who told you that?"

"Our washerwoman. I was taking poverty lessons from her. You can live a week on a pound of dried beans, a couple pounds of yucca and rice, a cake of raw sugar, some plantains: That's eighty pesos a week in the city, less in the country.

"What else do you need? A couple pair of cutoffs; you wash them in a stream now and then; dental care, you can't neglect that; the poor don't bother, I know, but I don't agree with that. Reduce things. You need a philosophy of things. What's dispensable, what's not…What was I saying? Oh, fluoride treatments, indispensable. Underwear, dispensable. Socks, I admit, have their function, unless you can dispense with shoes. Sandals, an excellent invention. Shaving, a waste of time, especially if you use dispensable blades. Running to the store for dispensable items is dispensable…"

"Go fuck yourself Willi. I'll shave my frigging legs if I feel like it," Blanche said.

Next day they bought tequila, rice, lentils, beans, salt, soap, kerosene, matches, seeds, candles, and took a bus up the mountain just before noon.

Kilómetro Veinticinco was a collection of three or four houses, a small store with a telephone exchange behind. Las Brumas was up the road about a half mile, overlooking the small settlement. They hiked up the hill. Several mud huts crowded against the road, sunbaked and crazed like old china. The road doubled back and Las Brumas came into sight, a wooden house painted white, with a red Eternit roof. The hillside was planted with coffee bushes shaded by plantain trees. Behind the house a pasture sloped steeply up. At the top was a cistern covered with a large concrete slab, and behind that another farmhouse.

Breathless, they stopped to rest. Leaning against the ferrous red gash where the road was carved into the mountainside, they put down the packs and gulped the thin air.

Another turn, and the drive up to the house ran off to the right. The house was surrounded by flowerbeds. The *Doña's* work, Carl thought. The two huts were at the back, off a dirt courtyard, substantial, concrete block structures with zinc roofs. In the doorway of one a girl stood watching them. Orlando's wife. She was awkwardly built with a large head, probably looked older than she was.

"*Buenas*," Carl said, and asked for Orlando.

"*Arriba*," she said, pointing up the slope.

Followed by her stare, they looked around. Opposite the huts was a stable with four stalls and a gleaming forage cutter. Coffee beans were spread to dry on the roof and a bougainvillea vine covered the sides. A wash was hung to dry over the vines; another soaked in a bucket.

Their hut was furnished with a wood stove, some pans and dishes, two beds with horsehair mattresses, and an old mahogany wardrobe. On the small front porch were a metal table and chairs.

"Excellent, excellent," Willi kept saying. "Nothing but what's necessary." They put away the groceries on two shelves over the stove and unrolled the bedrolls on the two beds. Willi took the back room and Carl and Blanche took the room off the kitchen. Willi started a fire in the stove with some kindling piled on the floor, but found this made the hut unbearably hot. He noticed that the girl had started to cook outside over a small kerosene stove; so, enduring her stares, he fabricated a barbecue with three cement blocks he found around back, and the wood stove's oven rack.

Carl walked up the hill and found Orlando coming down with the red cow and a black dog. He was tall, curly-haired, *mestizo*. "But The Doña isn't here," he kept saying, unable to imagine that any gringo would be visiting in the absence of doña Luz.

"To help with the work," Carl explained; but this idea seemed unacceptable to Orlando.

"I do the work. Where you from?" he said suddenly in English.

"Chicago."

"I live there," Orlando said.

"Where?"

"Texas, California. I dream all the time to go back."

Carl laughed.

"Why you come here? There is nothing here."

"Our house we were renting in Las Marias burned. The *Doña* offered us, the hut, Luciano's hut. We want to work, you show us…"

Orlando simply stared at Carl. "You hiding out from something?"

"Sort of."

"Ah," This, Orlando understood. The cow was pushed into the stable. "I milk her now."

Will left the fire and followed them in. "This is Willi." Carl said.

"Hiya." Orlando took an aluminum pan from a nail and began filling it. "You can't go back there?"

"We can go back," Willi said. "But we plan to live here."

"Nobody lives here that don't have to." He handed Willi the pan filled with milk. "Take. We don't drink much."

Blanche came in. She had washed her hair under the spigot, and put on shorts. Orlando stared at her and she gave him a frank look. Then he laughed.

Carl inspected the forage cutter's circular blade, oiled and gleaming. Under it was a bin of *caña brava* minced fine. An old saddle hung in the corner.

"Used to be a horse," Orlando said. "One of The *Doña's* nephews fell off and broke his neck." His eyes kept going to Blanche.

"This is Blanche," Carl said.

"Your woman or his?"

"Mine."

"I was a maintenance man in Texas for some Christian Science people. I take care of a cooling plant. They take care of me, but they don't like me to drink, smoke."

"Your wife should drink milk," Will said. The girl was pregnant. She stood in the doorway staring at them. Very young; fourteen or fifteen. "When is the baby?"

"January."

There wasn't enough firewood to finish the lentils. Willi moved them to Orlando's stove. They shared some fried plantains and sat around the oil lamp at the metal table drinking Cruz Verde. "We'll get a kerosene stove when we go down to Tuxpan next," Willi said. He was exhausted from his outdoor fire.

The darkness around them was filled with *cigarras* trilling and the mists had begun to descend. The girl, whose name was Miriam, washed up her pans at the spigot in the yard, using the red dust as an abrasive. No one had heard her speak beyond that first word.

"The *Doña* make us marry," Orlando said sheepishly, looking at her.

"A pressure cooker," Willi said. "Cultivating fork, cheese cloth, a colander, garden hose, sprinkler. I'll try bush beans behind the stable there, and transplant some of that yucca growing wild. Have you had any luck with corn?" he asked Orlando.

"Not much. No rains till December."

"That's what the hose is for?"

"We run water down for few days. Now is dried up."

"No, man, I've looked at that cistern," said Willi. It only needs cleaning.

He was trying to get Fidel on the short wave saved from the fire; but succeeded only in pulling in a powerful Bonaire gospel station.

The night was cold and damp as the clouds came down. Carl got up twice to close the shutters. Toward dawn he fell deeply asleep and woke late to the stove going, dispelling the damp and brewing coffee. Carl got up, wrapping himself in a poncho.

The clouds had begun to rise, though some remained caught in the bluish eucalyptus trees of the lower slopes; patches of weak sunlight filtered through. He stood out on the porch and watched Orlando come down from the boundary of The *Doña's* land. Together they pulled the steaming cow out of the stall. Orlando milked her and put her into the near pasture. They minced forage; what they had cut the night before was nearly gone. Carl went behind the stable to where the cane grew and cut down stalks with a machete, while Orlando put them through the hand-operated cutter. When Carl had filled the bin with stalks, he watched Orlando, then took a turn himself at the revolving blade, working until his arms ached.

Orlando went to bed then, after his night of patrolling the boundaries, and the girl, Miriam, came out to resume her silent washing by the pump in the yard.

Willi fried plantains and heated the milk for the coffee; then they walked down to the store below to buy bundles of firewood. The day was warming up and they sat at a wooden table in front of the little store drinking rum in chunky glasses. The storekeeper's wife had left for the market in Tuxpan before dawn and was back with a side of fatback, a beef heart, some soup bones. These she would retail to the poor shack dwellers around. She agreed to bring them a kerosene stove on her next trip, and sold them some bones and a beef heart.

"We won't come here often," Willi said, but Carl had a feeling they would.

They spent the rest of the morning transplanting the young yucca plants that had gone wild into a plot beside the stable. For lunch they had more fried plantains and beans. Carl fell asleep after, woke to the smell of Willi's *ocote* fire in the courtyard, bitter in his nostrils. Miriam was cooking too, over the petroleum stove on the porch. He had never been so aware of these processes of food gathering, preparation, and eating.

The late afternoon sun was warm, the air dry and clear. He wandered about the grounds, through vegetable gardens overgrown with *caña brava* and purple castor, swept and empty stables, plantain grove beside it, then a lean-to chicken house with shelves for roosting, fenced-in yard for scratching. There were some white leghorns with two or three baby chicks, a scrawny rooster. A leather-covered account book hung from a chain. Twenty-four leghorns, purchased Feb. 9, noted on the flyleaf. Inside were twenty-four columns with daily checks or zeros posted. Most of them seemed to lay daily at the beginning, less now. He went back and counted the chickens: seventeen.

"Leghorns," Orlando said behind him. "Don't lay much anymore, and no good to eat; *muy flacas.*" Carl moved on, through the plantain grove to the side of the big house which overlooked the valley.

The *Doña's* flowers were planted in neat rectangular beds outlined with stones, pebble paths between. *Margaritas*, gardenias, *veranera, inmortales*, he recognized; most he couldn't name. When she came, he would ask her. Would she come? He felt her presence in these colorful rectangles, these neat paths.

There was a glassed-in porch on this side of the house, with cement steps painted red. He went up and looked through the panes. There were some blocky red leatherette chairs at one end, a table covered in blue oilcloth, a bookcase with a few creamy paperbacks of the kind The *Doña* sent out to be bound in leather. The door was unlocked so he went in. He checked a few of the books to see, from the cut and uncut pages, where she had read. The French novels were mostly cut open; of the English titles she had read in their entirety only some essays. Back in Las Marias in her dim library they had been reading Henry Adams *Mt. San Michele and Chartres.* He recalled her grave school girl voice:

"Over the little church at Fenioux on the Charente,
 is a conical steeple an infidel might adore,"

Always she wanted him to stop her and correct her. Perhaps she will bring the book.

He continued around the house. There were rosebushes, a fig tree in green fruit, a bed of herbs: She had served him an infusion once made with *limoncillo* leaves. It helped the digestion.

The woman from the little store brought them back a kerosene stove next day which greatly simplified cooking and allowed it to be done indoors.

After that Carl did the errands. He went to the market on the early bus, arriving before seven. At one stall he bought rice, lentils, black beans; at another, tomatoes, and corn, which were their staples. Then, leaving his basket in the care of a lottery seller, he went to a cafe across the street and had a cup of *tinto* and a *mil hojas* pastry, and read one of the books from The *Doña's* library. Afterwards, wandering along Calle Tres de Mayo he bought little handcrafts: an enamel bowl, a set of pottery cups.

"But why do you buy these things?" Blanche complained, "weighing us down. It isn't as if we'd meant to come just here. To Kilómetro Veinticinco."

"Where, then?" he asked her, whose last residence before Carl's bedroom had been Boston Common. She was vexed from the start. Here was no buying of *cinco y seis* tickets to bet on horses, no cantinas that roared with talk. Carl, on the other hand finding he could sit in the shade under a ceiba tree and cut open the creamy pages of the *Doña* books here, as well as back in Las Marias, was content. Willi started painting again in egg tempera he mixed up himself.

And there was agriculture.

In November, they had their own lettuce, beans, and some yucca. The figs were ripe and Willi put them up in a syrup of *agua panela.* He learned to make white cheese from the left over milk, letting it stand three days, then pouring off the whey through a cloth and salting it heavily.

Carl brought back a new white rooster from the market, leading it on a leash. The hens were allowed to roost and six little leghorns were hatched.

Carl numbered them and noted their existence in a fresh page of the notebook hanging from the wall.

"I mean it isn't as if we meant to come exactly here," Blanche said from the bed, watching Carl hang up a weaving bought from an Indian claimed to have walked here from La Virginia. A monkey with a triangular green face and a tree. "The monkey is bigger than the tree," said Blanche. "Crazy." She was drinking *agave* tea.

"Where is it you want to go then?" he asked.

"How do I know, if we just sit here on this mountain."

Carl sat down on the bed. "You oughtn't to drink that stuff."

"It does no harm. Only the *mescal* harms. It makes me feel good, bigger than this mountain. Like that monkey, bigger than the tree. If only we hadn't sold the car, Carl, Carl."

"You want to stay with me?"

"No... yes."

"You'd have left me if we were back there?"

"Maybe, maybe not."

"You're free. We said we'd be free."

"Oh, Carl, Carl."

"What do you want? What?"

"Hold me."

"You shouldn't..."

"Hold me!" She was naked, perspiring. They rocked together. "I want..."

"What? What?"

"Help me, Carl, help me. I'm disappearing." They lay together, perspiring.

"What do you do with your old lady?" she whispered.

"Nothing. Talk."

"What do you talk about?"

"Churches."

"Churches. Oh, hold me hold me, don't move . . . Yes, yes, it's a nice monkey. His face is green and he's bigger than the tree. Tell me, tell me about churches. What church do you talk about?"

"Chartres. It has two towers. Built in different centuries. The older one is finer."

"Why?"

"It solves the problem of changing from a square to a hexagon ."

"Ah, is that what The *Doña* worries about?"

"She's a good woman."

"Am I good?"

"Yes. I wish you could be happy."

"I can't, Carl; that's what I'm trying to tell you."

"Why, why?"

"It's death. I feel death here."

"What death?"

"That child that fell off the horse. I don't know… the hens. Death, Carl."

"I don't understand. An accident. A couple hens…"

"It's here. It's why they don't come."

"They'll come."

"Your old lady talks about churches. That's funny. She's old, Carl…"

"Not so old. Younger than him."

"Forty at least. She can't have children."

"She's good, good."

"How, good, how?"

"…takes care of us all. Orlando, Miriam, the gardens, the nephews, us."

"Old, Carl. They're thousands of years older than we are. Don't you feel it?"

"Maybe."

"You like it. You like to read her old books. But you don't see. It's death."

"She brings up his brother's children, he said, "They have nothing. She sends them to good schools."

"And don Rafa brings up the children of the *telegrafista* down in the village."

"Who says that."

"Everyone knows they're his." She held out the cup to him. "Drink."

He sipped the musty tasting infusion. Felt nothing. Like Willi, he preferred Cruz Verde.

Each day was sunny as the previous one. It was the *verano*. The pastures were brown, and above *Los Franceses*, fires blackened the mountain. One of Carl's young reds died, and three more of the old Leghorns.

But, at the end of November, the big house was opened up. The daughter of the *Telegrafista* came up to cook and Orlando's wife moved over to help in the kitchen. A week later The *Doña* arrived with *doña* Bertha and the four nephews, who slept in the bunk beds in the annex to the house. They would stay through Christmas.

Three large meals were prepared daily. Occasionally, when the kitchen in the big house became too hot, dishes were baked in Orlando's oven and carried over to the house. Sometimes, the remains of a meal, a *flan*, or a dish of baked plantains would be sent out to them.

The *Doña's* English lessons resumed at ten every morning. They met on the glass-enclosed porch at the back of the house overlooking the garden with the gravel paths.

"Have you everything you need?" she asked him in her careful English on the first day.

"Oh, yes. The woman at the *abasto* brings us supplies from Tuxpan, and I go once a week."

"You must go with Juan while we are here."

"Thank you."

"They charge too much, at the *abasto*. I know you have limited…and I wish to pay you the hundred pesos weekly for the lessons."

"But it is too much," he said, "We are living here without paying."

"No, no, I wish to pay."

"You are very kind."

Orlando's woman brought a tray with *café tinto* and some white rolls. She stared at Carl, unable to comprehend that someone who cleaned out the hen house was also received here in the big house and served by herself.

"The little boys come here to recover their health on the vacation. The air of the mountains opens the appetite. We do not have the change of season, so the body suffers unless one changes the altitude."

"It is very beautiful here."

"Yes, when it suns."

"When the sun shines," he corrected her.

"When the sun shines as now there is nowhere more beautiful. When it rains it is a sad climate some say."

"And you?"

"It is my home. My family is of Tuxpan. It is pleasing to me, the high, the cold, the black pines, the white houses…"

He watched her face. It was pale as usual, but animated. She had been wearing black since she arrived. It seemed that a cousin had died, and the women in the family had adopted *luto*. The black had shocked him when she first arrived, and made her look haggard, but today she had thrown a blue sweater over her shoulders and was wearing a pair of slacks for the country. He told her she looked well.

"The place where one is from, where one has been happy," she said. "It is a climate for serious men they say. My grandfather wore always a black hat and a cloak. He could recite all of Robledo by heart."

"And why did you leave?"

"I marry. Don Rafa dislikes here. He has arguments with the priests at the seminary where they sent him."

"But it must bore you;" she turned her fine eyes on him, "a woman's life."

"No, no, why ever?" he cried, embarrassing her.

"The cow does well," she said, turning the subject.

"Yes, yes."

"She is old, but she does well, yes; when we are living in the city, drinking the milk from the store that one never knows what they put in it, I say to don Rafa, 'What a grateful thing it is to come here and drink the milk of a cow that is…how do you say, *una vaca conocida?*'"

"A cow one is acquainted with."

"Yes, yes," she laughed. "A cow one is acquainted with." She looked him timidly in the face. "You will go back to your country one day, I am sure."

"No, no, never to that."

"That what?"

"That waiting to begin. Nothing could begin."

"But one's county!" she said.

"One's county…one's county drops bombs where there is nothing to bomb. Everyone knows it is a disgrace, and yet it has gone so far it cannot be stopped, or anyone say it's been for nothing."

"Still, it will be over one day. You will go back."

"I cannot for now, in any case."

"I cannot understand it," she said. "To have such a dislike for one's country. We criticize ourselves all the time, as you notice…my husband. Yet we never do not love."

One of her small nephews had come into the room.

"I am afraid it is a custom here," she said, caressing the child, "for sons of wealthy families to buy. . . how shall I say? To pay a sum to avoid the conscription."

"I could have done that," Carl said. "That is I could have stayed . . . in school; but I'm glad I didn't. It is better, as Willi says, to reject, to make one's life a statement."

"I do not understand, I'm afraid," she said. The child leaned heavily against her, pressing for her attention. "How can one reject one's entire . . . that is to say . . . one's life?"

"Do you despise me?"

"Despise you? But hardly know you," she said, innocent of how she injured him.

Doña Berta came in and called him to her. "He is no trouble," said doña Luz, allowing the child to slip from her lap. Berta, who had eight children, was a small woman with a narrow dark face. She was married to a brother of don Rafa's who was relatively poor. At eleven every morning she played hearts on the verandah with *misia* Eulalia and her daughter from up the hill.

"I don't know," Carl said. "I can't explain it, but my first *positive* feeling in these past four or five years has been deciding to come here..." He felt slightly off balance, having been interrupted by the child's mother as he was about to tell her more...the waiting, the impossibility of beginning a life when everything depended on a draft number, but, as she had said, she barely knew him.

"But," she said to Carl, "You have ruin your career, your life. What is there for you here?"

"This place. Useful work."

"I'm afraid it is not a...how you say...a serious farm. The soil is poor. It is for the air we come, the flowers..." She moved a gray porcelain dove to a high shelf out of reach of the child. "Still, your mother, she is sad. It is such a distance. I mean, to live in a foreign country."

"You learn a foreign language," he said.

"Ah, but it is only to travel as a tourist, to read, perhaps. You think it is useless, that I should rather play hearts with the others?"

"No, no! I admire you. You are altogether admirable!"

"An idle woman."

"No, you must read! And you might travel; but you said you never would again."

"Never as I once did."

"How is that?"

"Young. Alone." She laughed.

"What is funny?"

"It is an old family joke. An old aunt, very rich, she never left Envigado. They had a farm there, a very old-fashioned family. One year her husband made great preparations, took a train at La Victoria and a ship at Los Olmos, and went to Europe. My aunt stayed in Envigado and crocheted her tablecloths and played games of *tute* and drank her chocolate at eleven. She sighed when she thought of her husband. 'The poor man. Alone in Paris,' she would say."

"Ah, yes, yes!" he laughed. How charming she was when she told these stories.

"Alone in Paris, ah yes. Will you have a biscuit?"

"Thank you."

"It is a terrible thing, the bombing. You are not mistaken I hope," she said. "It is to be heard every evening on the radio."

"Ah, then I suppose it must be true, the radio." She turned her gray eyes on him. Charming woman. What had produced her? What slow education, what long breeding produced these reticences, these occasional drolleries, this deep gaze?

Blanche washed the way Miriam did, soaping the clothes with a green naptha bar and spreading them on the grassy verge of the courtyard to bleach; then holding them under the spigot and stretching them over the *veranera* vines to dry. They often washed together, but the girl never spoke. If I had a child in me I'd be the same, like a bitch in the sun, Blanche thought.

After the washing the clothes, she washed her hair and shaved her legs. Carl brought her blades despite Willi's desire to let all hair grow. She let her armpits sprout, but not her legs. Then, with a sprig of *veranera*, she cleaned under her toenails, between her teeth, into her ears, around her clitoris, sniffing herself with pleasure. A dun-colored iguana watched her. She was hidden from curious eyes by the *veranera*, but she didn't care who looked at her. The burning *ocote* reminded her of autumn. Here there was no autumn. Only some weather the winds brought over the mountain.

Nearby, Willi worked dung into the soil and set out his tomato and pepper seedlings. The seeds Luciano gave him had begun to sprout: Amaranth, ancient food of the Aztecs. He planned to upgrade the fodder with it, use leaves and beans in soup. It was a nearly forgotten food according to Luciano. Willi had written his father to research it.

He noted the rain clouds hung over the *cordillera*. Let them come soon, he thought, sprinkling the seedlings. Just past noon, he used the new shit hole behind the plantains, covered his contribution to the collection of night soil with loose clay. It was preferable to the smelly latrine. After, he took a shower in the stall behind the stable, washing his cutoffs and his T shirt at the same time. The red clay stains didn't come out completely. He hung the clothes over the wall of the shower stall to dry and pulled on a clean shirt and a clean pair of cutoffs hanging there. They were stiff and scratchy and the pockets had fallen off, but serviceable. He passed Blanche, behind the *veranera*, smoking. She handed him her little clay pipe. It was rather good stuff, bought in the Café Media Luna from an old *marijuanero*.

"You never draw me anymore."

"I'll draw you now." He went to the hut for his pad.

"Shall I take off my things?"

"No."

"Why? I always used to in Las Marias."

"All right. May as well get all the joints and muscles."

She stepped out of her shorts and pulled off her jersey. "Is that all you get?"

"Frankly, no."

"Is that true, Willi?"

"I feel like any other man."

"Then why don't you want me?"

"I control myself."

"Why bother?"

"Like Gandhi, I use the energy for other things."

"Did he draw naked women?"

"He took young women in his bed and never touched them."

"Stuff!"

"Truth."

"How do you want me?"

"Bend your left knee and raise yourself on your elbow."

"What if they touched him?"

"Who?"

"Gandhi. What if the women touched him?"

"He didn't say. Put your arm across your belly."

"Like this?"

"Yeah. Relax it more; spread your fingers."

Carl and The *Doña* walked among the *margaritas*, sat under the fig tree. She had adopted *semiluto* for the country, which meant she wore the black slacks with a figured blouse. She alternated between one with black dots and another with a faint purple flower pattern. She carried today two gardenias in her right hand. Like the Virgin, he thought, who carried lilies, or rather a scepter entwined with lilies as a sign of her power, according to Henry Adams.

"How I have missed this, here," she said. "We have not come for over two years. One of my nephews…"

"I know," Carl said. "Orlando told us."

"He was thirteen. As a young child he was often ill. He had asthma and he was overweight." She began pulling the dead blossoms off of the bush, throwing them into a pile of compost. *Flores marchitas.*

"But he had the most loving nature. We thought he would go through life like that: a little lazy, without many friends. His mother liked him least of her children, I'm afraid, but he was my favorite. Always he came to me with his troubles.

"'I'm going to be a better student,' he said to me one day, and began to bring me his lessons." She sat on a bench at the end of the garden. "Then he lost his weight; he exercised more; became more like other children."

The youngest nephew came out of the house and ran into the garden.

"He was beginning life. A beautiful boy. 'I'll be an engineer like *tio* Rafa,' he'd say."

"Will there be *cojetes* for Christmas?" the child demanded.

"What is that?" Carl asked.

"That is fire arms."

"Fire arms!"

"No, no! Artificial fire..."

"Ah, fireworks."

"To celebrate the Child's birth. But there are lovely things too, you shall see, at Christmas..."

"Don't talk like that!" the little boy pulled her back into the house.

The dry season was lasting into the fourth month, though the storm clouds hung over the *cordillera*. The grass on the mountains burned palely in the daylight, leaving charred smudges. When the rains came the slopes turned green in a day, Orlando said, and the cattle fed on the new grass. But the trees would not grow back, so the soil ran off and eventually the slope would turn barren and the only cactus would grow.

Carl lay under the mosquito net slitting the pages of his book with a kitchen knife.

"Why do you have to do that?" Blanche asked.

"It's quarto edition."

"Where do they publish books like that?"

Carl looked in the front of the book. "Barcelona."

"Oh, her books would be posh."

He didn't answer.

"What else do you talk to your *doña* about?"

"I can't talk to her."

"Why not?"

"She doesn't know who I am." He threw aside the book. "Oh, we speak; but if we lived here fifty years she wouldn't know me. We haven't been properly introduced."

"You love her."

He didn't answer.

"You give me a pain, Carl."

"I'm sorry."

After he had fallen asleep, she got up and sat in the kitchen. The sound of Orlando's whistle approached down the hillside. She went out and watched him come into view in the light from his lantern. He was wearing a rain poncho, carrying something inside it.

"What do you have?"

He showed her: a little ocelot.

"Oh, I love him!" she said.

"You have him. He is yours."

"Oh, see! A kitty cat, an ickle puddy!"

"They can get dangerous."

"No, no, he'll love me."

"Tell me something." He sat on the steps next to her. "You married to him in there?"

"No."

"I'm married. The *Doña* make us marry," he said.

"I know. Maybe you'll have a son. It's nice to have a son."

"I already have two."

"Where?"

"Down at. Kilómetro Veinticinco. Everywhere there is someone willing to give me a son. Except the ladies of the Christian Science. They give me Bible lessons..."

"Bible lessons?" Blanche was starting to giggle.

"Over there, in your country, I work for Christian Science Church. Handyman. They are good people. This lady she take an interest in me. She was thirty-two; she does not believe in sex before marriage."

"Oh Gawd!" She put a hand over her mouth so as not to wake Carl.

"But everything, we do...everything; except for putting it in."

"Oh Jesus, God!"

"She love it, all the other things. 'Aye, Orlando!' she holler when I bring her. 'There is no one like you...'"

"Stop, stop!" Blanche howled. "I'm wetting my . . . I'm wetting my pants!"

"She lick me, she bite me. Everything, everything but putting it in..."

"I'm wetting them. Oh, oh . . ." She stood up.

"*Asquerosa!*" He leaped away from her.

"Oh, my God, on my God! I haven't done that since sixth grade."

"*Puerca!*"

"Oh dear, oh dear!" she was dissolved.

"Fix yourself!" he yelled. "Don't just sit there!"

She jumped up and ran behind the bougainvillea, pulled off shorts and panties and flung them over the vine. "So what happened? The Bible lady?" she said, stepping into a pair of clean panties she'd hung to dry earlier.

"Oh, she drive me mad. I have to smoke, drink. They take away my job; then I am good for nothing. I live on women. I am owing the telephone company, the electric company. They make me to leave. Ach. I come back here and The *Doña* take care of me. Aye, women!" He stood up. I must go... My rounds. Don Rafa should not catch me here."

"And I can keep the kitty cat?" She buried her face in his fur.

A day toward the end of November, The *Doña* came in the car with baskets. Carl went out to help her.

"No, no it is no matter. I will leave everything here for Orlando." She put two baskets down, held on to the other:

"Are you well? You look pale," she said."

"No, no. I am perfectly well." He walked beside her along the gravel path bordered by *margaritas.* They paused at a gardenia bush, and she stooped to pick off the browning flowers.

"What is this?" he asked, pointing to a plant with shiny dark green leaves in the shape of broad spears.

"That is *columna.*"

He took out a notebook and wrote the name together with a sketch of the leaf.

"It likes shade. That's why I've put it here under the fig tree." She looked at him gravely: "You wished to speak to me about something?"

"Well, there is the matter of a pig . . . Willi asked if I would speak to you. He would like us to buy a sow to mate."

"Ah, we used to have pigs."

She picked some *margaritas,* then straightened up. "A pig, yes, we shall see."

"It would be our responsibility. It's care, I mean."

"Yes, of course. One used to be slaughtered every year for Christmas."

"*El puerco conocido,*" he said.

"Ah, yes," she laughed: "The pig one is acquainted with. I would never acquaint myself with a pig that I may later, how you say? Roast." She handed him some of the margaritas. "Your wife will like?"

"Yes, thank you. You are so good...so..."

"A quite ordinary woman," she said firmly.

"No, not ordinary, I . . . think…"

"Please."

"I think of you. You are always in my…"

"No, no!"

"Please, I must. I…I admire you. I admire you in the most extraordinary way."

"But you must not."

"Oh, God, oh God! Forgive me!"

"It would be wise to go in," she said. "The sun… "

"Forgive me."

"It is no matter."

He followed her: "If you would just allow me to explain. I don't mean to upset you…"

"Please." She put a hand on his arm and he caught it up in his.

"No, no!"

He released her. "Forgive me,"

"We will not speak of it more." She moved toward the house.

"I can say it better, if you will allow me."

"No, no, you must not!"

"I…I think how everything here… how everything you touch… you care for . . . I think, just let me, just let me be one of these things you care for, like this garden…"

"You must not speak this way."

"How can I help? How can one help?"

"One can always help."

"I mean if you knew how my mind goes around, how I cannot help observing how no one *sees* you as I do… "

"God sees. It is for God to see."

"Oh, God! Don't talk of God. I mean who is it says I cannot feel this way? Is it God?"

"I must go in," she said.

"Forgive me, then, at least that. Let us be like before."

She smiled. "You have a young wife."

"Yes, yes." He had been tempted to tell her they were not married, but it would have shocked her. Or, he wondered, would she would have forced them before a priest? But no, he thought bitterly, she didn't care enough for that.

"I shall speak to *don* Rafa about the pig. One must go in now, out of the sun." She picked up the basket.

He made a new resolve and found it gave him some peace. I will *watch* her, he thought. No one will know it. I will simply watch her. He imagined this watching as something which might happen over an uncounted number of years. It would be a focus for his life.

He was very careful of her for a week. The lessons became as before. She didn't invite him to walk in the garden, though she was as cordial as ever when they had the coffee and biscuits after the lesson. He had noted that she went every Thursday with Juan the driver in the car, carrying with her baskets full of canned goods. Finally he asked if he might go with her. She hesitated, then consented; so the following Thursday he was ready when Juan brought out the baskets.

"But they will tire you, my little visits," said *doña* Luz. "They can be of no interest to a young man like you."

"I wish to go," Carl repeated, helping her put into each basket the cellophane bags of Fideos Lux, the black beans, the jars of fig preserves, the boxes of *petits beurres.*

"You will not speak again of the matters you...the other day."

"No, no, never again," he said.

Juan drove them, down to Kilometro Veintitres, behind the *telefónico,* a rutted track which threaded a narrow canyon and climbed halfway up the opposite slope, where they got out and walked, the baskets carried by Juan and six or seven little boys who clamored: "*La Doña, viene La Doña.*"

The first shack was that of an aged woman tended by a mute boy. The basket was placed on the stoop and emptied by the boy. "*Bendita mujer,*" said the woman. Her eyes were filmed over; she seemed to have only sidelong vision, in which she held The *Doña.*

"Give them the Coca Cola," the woman said to the boy, and he held a bottle out to Carl, who stood uncomfortably in the dusty yard finishing the warm flat drink as the boy stood watching him as if administering a dose. *Doña* Luz refused hers, asking instead for a cutting of an unusual philodendron rooting in a pail on the stoop.

Walking on, with the little plant wrapped in her handkerchief, she warned him to ask for juice if they wanted to bring him a drink, not Coca Cola; it was too expensive.

Doña Mercedes, in the next cottage, expected them to enter and sit on two rusted chrome chairs, either side of a glass-topped coffee table on which was an arrangement of artificial flowers. The floor was swept earth; and, high on one whitewashed wall, hung an oleograph of the Sacred Heart.

"*Mi hija menor,*" said doña Mercedes, indicating the pretty girl sitting on a brocade settee next to a young man. "And Gonzalo, her sweetheart." Gonzalo stood up and offered a hand to Carl. The girl sat mute through the introduction. She was dressed up in a three-piece outfit.

"He is from Cartago," said the mother, meaning the young man.

"Ah, Cartago," said The *Doña*, accepting a glass of *badea* pulp and a cracker. "We pass through Cartago coming from Las Marias." A bit of cracker fell from her lap and she bent over to recover it from the earth floor.

She is a lady, thought Carl. She passes the ultimate test of ladyhood, making this polite talk in this appalling place.

"There is the sugar mill as well," said *doña* Mercedes.

"I work in the sugar mill," said the young man.

The girl said nothing. She was elaborately painted and sat as if not to disturb the fall of her taffeta skirt.

"They will marry in February," said the mother.

"I congratulate you."

"Will you have a Coke?" the woman inquired of Carl.

"No, no!"

Carl stared at the barbed and bleeding heart of Christ hung high on the opposite wall. The girl had not spoken a word. Women, here, found their voices only in middle age.

They went on. A crippled woman with three infants had no oleographs on the wall, or plastic flowers on the table. The single room contained two rusted cots, a petroleum stove, a table covered in oilcloth, and two benches.

"The pain is terrible, *Doña*. I walk all bent over." Her spine was twisted, causing the hip on which the youngest child rode to protrude grotesquely.

"Dr. Escobar Soto will see you. He is my own doctor."

But what could he do about this? What can anyone do? Carl thought.

"You take the silver bus, I believe, from the…"

"Oh, I know about buses, *Doña*."

Carl emptied the basket on to one of the benches. They climbed the rest of the way up the hill by a narrow track. "These next you will find rather educated people. They are exiles, from over the border. Don Sergio is an organizer of strikes. Sonia teaches in the school."

They entered a tiny house that was whitewashed inside and out, with gauze curtains in the windows to keep out flies. A robust young woman embraced *doña* Luz and shook Carl's hand: "Sergio is not here." This seemed a relief to *doña* Luz. She took a seat; at a metal table where two children studied.

"Greet The *Doña* nicely," said Sonia. Girl and boy stood up and gave their hands to *doña* Luz and to Carl.

"*Y usted…*" she said to Carl, her face full of humor. "We have heard about you." She brought them coffee, sitting down herself and pulling her coarse black hair away from her face. Unlike The *Doña*, Carl thought, she is sure of being a good woman; her children sit before her, obviously healthy, polite, studious.

"They are spreading tacks on the road today, in support of the truckers," Sonia said. "You must tell Juan to tie twigs in front of the wheels,"

"Today?"

"Yes, they were around last night, between here and La Verenjena. Didn't you notice?"

"Nothing."

"David," she said to the boy. "Go tell Juan." The boy ran.

"So," she said to Carl, "What do you think of us here?"

He wasn't prepared for her directness. "It's all very new," he said. "I am very interested…"

"Nothing is new to me," she said. "It is all the same as before. I never knew if he comes home. Yet we are well here. They accept my certificate. I am paid full salary now. And my brother comes and will add to the house, two rooms, a kitchen and a room for himself. He's a quiet man. He'll come home evenings."

"You're a good woman, Sonia," said The *Doña*.

"Yes . . . though I don't baptize my children. I know you are thinking that."

"Perhaps, if one is frank, yes."

Carl noted the absence of oleographs. The only things to hang on the wall were two machetes.

"I am aware that a wife must obey a husband," said *doña* Luz gently. "This is a delicious coffee."

It was delicious, and Carl drank it with guiltless pleasure.

"Our own beans. We sell, now, the eggs as well." She led them out to the yard. Under a mango tree was a coop made of derelict boards, covered with scraps of Eternit roofing, on which were spread coffee beans.

Carl followed the two women up a hill, Sonia's strong calves just in front of him. "My place," she said when they reached the top. There was a bench and an arbor of woodroses. They sat down, Carl on the ground, at the feet of *doña* Luz.

"You see the valley from here," Sonia said. "All the way to Kilómetro Diez y Ocho."

"But it's lovely," said Luz, clapping her hands. "Truly!"

"Sergio laughs at me. 'Here, I come and pray you will not be killed,' I tell him. 'I lose, through you, my family, my homeland, my religion. I can at least pray they do not take you.'"

"My dear," said doña Luz.

"I will be strong, yes, I will. He will come home tonight, like all other nights. "It will be some other day, some ordinary day when I am not expecting it, he won't come."

"No, no, you mustn't say such things." The *Doña* embraced her while she sat straight and still, her eyes closed.

"Forgive me, please."

Sonia wiped her eyes with her apron, and led them back down the hill. She gave them two papayas. Her face was empty, now and calm. She gave Carl her hand. "You come again."

"I will," he said, "With much pleasure!"

Juan had tied brushes of twigs in front of each tire. Some of the trucks they passed had devised the same safeguard. Several were of the road with blowouts.

A pair of Hampshire pigs was purchased. Male and female. They were sleek and black with a white belt running down both front legs. Willi pointed out the tightly curled tails, sign of health. He had learned something of pigs when he spent summers with his uncle. They would be mated. Willi built them a fenced yard behind the stable, and no attempt was made to become acquainted with them except by Blanche, who liked to lean over the boards and tickle the sow with a branch from a coffee bush. *Don* Rafa bought a new notebook and hung it on a nail to record their weight gain. The male weighed 172 pounds and the female, 160 pounds. They ate the leftover tortillas and the egg shells from breakfast and drank milk mixed with *agua panela*. At night Willi boiled up a mash for them on the kerosene stove. If the mating took, there would be tender piglet to roast by next July according to Willi's calculations.

The rains held off, however, and Willi had to leave off the pigs' daily bath with Orvus Soap. The bruised clouds hung back behind the *cordillera*, and fires crisped the dry mountainsides.

A morning when Carl was reading with doña Luz, the girl Miriam announced that there was a Virgin on the mountainside.

"*Pero qué!*" exclaimed The *Doña*, starting up from her chair.

"You see it from here," said Miriam, motioning them to the center of the patio. "No, no, you don't. From the kitchen patio better." They followed her through the kitchen to the washing patio. "There," she pointed. "I saw her first." It was the most Carl had ever heard her speak.

"Above the track to Palomares," said Olga, her hands deep in corn *masa*.

"The fires will take her, they're saying. A priest has been sent for."

Carl squinted against the sun. Something bluish, tent shaped, moving slightly in the wind; though there was no wind there below...

"It is a hysteria," said don Rafa, discovering them.

"It isn't clear, obviously it's something," The *Doña* said.

"A Pisanista flag, left over from the last election," said don Rafa.

"Away up there, *mi hijo*? Who would carry such a thing up there? There isn't even a path.

"If one could only see clearer. The opera glasses, have we them somewhere?" asked The *Doña*.

"They have looked with a glass already. You do not see clearer, only larger," stated Olga.

"I think in the bookshelf." Doña Luz went into the house.

"Some people were going up there with *Padre* Elias from San Fernando," said Olga. "But they are afraid . . . the fire."

"A hysteria," said don Rafa,

The *Doña* returned with the opera glasses and handed them to don Rafa:

"A little look, here, a flag, I will wager; yes, a flag; it is quite clear."

Doña Luz took back the glasses, refocused them silently. Finally, she said: "It isn't clear; it does seem to turn and..."

"The flag, it is blowing in the wind," said Rafa.

"We shall ask our gringo here." He handed the glasses to Carl. "He has no interest either way. He will approach the matter in a cool, scientific way. Look, you; very fine opera glasses from Paris."

Carl focused the glasses on the mountainside. The shape swept close, and for a moment he saw what might have passed for a Virgin; but the truth was it wasn't clear, larger, but not clearer.

"So?" said Rafa.

"It could be a flag and it could be a figure," Carl said to everyone's dissatisfaction. "That is, it's blue, it moves."

"There, you see, an objective statement. scientific mind," said don Rafa. "In this country we have not the scientific mind."

After supper, Rafa brought out a bottle of Cruz Verde:

"To the scientific impulse, eh?" he said, tossing off a glassful.

"And now we have this Virgin, ach!"

"It is odd," Carl said.

"What's that?"

"How it's not clearer with the glasses."

"Hah! Now we have our gringo corrupted by kitchen maids, by my old lady."

"But...you shouldn't."

"Shouldn't...?"

"Speak of her...in that way."

"Ah, hah!" Don Rafa examined him closely in the lamplight. "So, you are an admirer of my wife, eh? So, yes, yes, my wife is one of the, shall we say, *flowerings* of our feudal state. One must admire her, but one must look also at the state, at the understructure, at what is bearing her up, so to speak: a lot of poor devils carrying loads on their backs, eh? You must know that."

"Well, if you speak of that; what is bearing one up, what is bearing anyone up? What is bearing me up?" Carl stammered. "Wars, legitimized industrial greed." His face flamed.

"Your 'legitimized industrial greed', I'm sure it produces some charming ladies too."

"Never, never anyone like her," Carl said.

"So, you have experienced them all! Hah, but I must tell you something about my lady. She is my first cousin. We marry so the money stays in the family." Don Rafa poured another round. "Well, tell me then what is so extraordinary that you find?"

"I can't explain."

"Ah, it is some kind of mystery! Mysteries, Virgins. How old are you?"

"Twenty-three."

"Twenty-three. At twenty-five, I was plotting assassinations." *Don* Rafa wandered outside the circle of the lantern, returned:

"Tell me then, what is this something you find, in this ferrous piece of mountainside, I married to keep in the family? Is it something to do with virgins? "

"Back in the Thirteenth Century the Virgin was considered Mistress of the Seven Liberal Arts," Carl said.

Ah, a medieval young man." Rafa waved toward the mountain: "That, that up there, if it is a virgin, it's an old dead battery, an old dead battery of a virgin!"

"The people down at the abasto say the rains come to save her," said Orlando.

"Ha ha ha! The Virgin or the Pisanista flag!" burst from don Rafa.

Carl brought Willi to meet Sonia. They rode up on the afternoon bus.

"This woman is a teacher, you say?"

"Yes."

"It's your intellectual proletariat. Teachers here, I'm told, only make menial wage. Their only resource is revolution."

"And they have some crops."

"Yes. The coffee crop looked to be farther along than ours."

"So it is all here…The Maoist elements. The agricultural base. The political awareness."

Willi's excitement reminded Carl of Carl Marx's frustrated desire to encounter a genuine German Socialist.

He watched out the window of the bus for the nearest stop where they could get out and walk up the hill to the farm. As he remembered it was just beyond Kilómetro Treinta where Juan had turned off and headed up a rutted road as far as the Mercedes would go. Yes, here was the little crossroads, with the pharmacy and the telephone exchange with the little *abasto* even smaller than their own little village.

They found Sergio at home that day, sorting coffee beans with his son. Sonia gripped Carl's hand and smiled. "You see he came," she said.

Sergio got a bottle of Ron Viejo from the kitchen and brought it out to the table on the front porch. He was a square, sturdy man like his wife, his smooth, beardless face reddened over the cheekbones by the altitude.

"So, you stay with don Rafa, eh? I have met him. One of the old Liberals. One of the Great Talkers. They couldn't even kill El Cóndor," said Sergio.

"The mountain will defeat the plain. Here in the *cordillera* is our future, our party, our leaders. The city cannot corrupt them. We wait. But we prepare…

"Listen, listen, I will show you." Sergio got up and led them through a small back room and out through the dusty back yard, up the hill Carl had climbed before. He parted a thicket of vine, pulled: away a pallet of weathered boards over which a mesh of pine branches had been stapled. Behind, a tunnel had been dug into the red clay.

Sergio pulled out a crate and pried it open. It was filled with rifles wrapped in rags.

"M-14s," he said, unwrapping the greasy cloth. "Fires 7.62 millimeter cartridges; has a range up to seven hundred meters. And this." He dug out another. "Grenade launcher. Aluminum barrel. Has a range between a hand grenade and a mortar."

He pulled out another crate and unwrapped a pair of machine guns. "M-16's, modified for automatic fire.

"Where do you get them?" Willi asked.

"The AKM's come in the powdered milk."

"What?"

"The *Centros Rurales* receive aid shipments. I tell you this because you are exiles like us?"

"Yes, yes," Willi said.

"I take the risk of trusting you, right?"

"Yes, yes."

"The rice and the milk are sent in from Eastern Europe, then they are distributed by the *Rurales*. these weapons, are hidden in caves in thirty-four districts. We avoid concentrations of weapons, same as we avoid troop concentrations. Disseminated *focus*. We go on with our lives, but there are periods of training. We have seventeen focos. We are the closest to the city. It is, here, most dangerous to operate.

"Some weapons come also from the *cuartel*," Sergio said, rewrapping the machine guns in rags. "Sabotage, desertions take place. We surrounded a company on maneuvers a month ago, took over a hundred M-16's. Since then we've had to be very careful." He pushed away the crate of weapons, pulled out a cardboard box: "My books."

Carl knelt to look. There was <u>The Marx Engels Reader</u>, Debray, a quarto edition of Zola's *Germinal* on creamy paper like The *Doña's* books.

"I must hide them now. It becomes more dangerous." Sergio pushed the boxes back in and straightened up. "You were right to leave there," he said. "It is because of that that I show you this. It is all one struggle, yes?"

They walked back down the hill. "You say nothing, especially to *don* Rafa. He is a good man. He was in prison in the days of Salazar they say. It is only, he talks, and the time for that is over.

"'The urge to destroy is also the creative urge,' Bakunin said. The Liberal's parliamentary democracy is nothing but a fraud which the upper class uses to dominate the masses. These gentlemen we have now in the Palacio de Armas will perpetuate themselves until the devil knows."

They sat under a silkcotton tree with the bottle of Ron Viejo.

"Our other weapon is the strikes. But this we must leave mostly to our brothers in the city. At the end, though, at the end, we will all come together as it was in Petrograd. It must ripen."

"You have a good soil here," Willi said, nudging at an ant hill with his sandal.

"Yes, volcanic ash. Better than over your way. Life is good. My children grow; my wife has her profession; but one lives for ideas or one is a brute."

"Ach! Ideas!" cried Sonia, who stooped nearby, sorting coffee beans.

"For justice, *mi amor*," he said.

She bent over her beans, not answering.

The bruised clouds remained just behind the mountains and the rains didn't come, but the Virgin remained, untouched. "Run, see, Olga," Berta said every afternoon at cards.

"See if she's still there."

"Still up there, eh, turning the heads of kitchen girls," said Rafa, sitting on their stoop. "You get this talk of miracles when a religion is new and when it's in decay. A compound in putrefaction gives up its elements. It's simple chemistry. It all begins in miracles and goes out in miracles." Carl sat staring up at the fires. Willi sucked a lime.

"But who's to do something!" Carl erupted.

"Yes, years, we talked, I admit. Precious little we did. Best to shut up. My wife distributes her baskets; I suppose that's something. But it's never going to end the misery of this mountain."

"Trouble is," said Willi, "No one's seen what could be made of it."

"Of what?" asked don Rafa. *"La miseria?* What can be made of it but more misery…?"

"No, no, limits, possessing only what's necessary. Where do the diminishing returns begin in possessing? Knowing that," Willi insisted

"Ah, well, asceticism. It's an elite understands such things.

"You give money to one of these *miserables.* Does he spend it on wholesome food or necessities? No, he shows off with a banquet, spends it all on drink and *bizcochos,*" said Rafa.

"Maybe the fault lies in the money," Willi said.

"How so?"

"Money creates diffuse desires, unreality," Willi said.

"But can we to do away with it? It's there and everyone wants it," Carl asked.

"By faith,"

"Faith in what?"

"In this lime," Willi said, holding one up. "In its reality, it's nourishment, its beauty. There's no use hoarding it; it will spoil."

"And who's to be prophet of this faith?"

"Its prophet will come. For every truth, there's never lacked a prophet."

"You're right about faith of course," said Rafa. "Nothing's ever accomplished without passion. We're an age short of passion, of symbol; whatever's up there…Virgin, well she's dying; Pisanista flag, well they lost in '59. I carried their banner through the streets once myself. Pisano inspired a certain . . . an honest man, you know, you had to call him that. Bad stammer. Poignant that he'd stand up in public at all, put himself forward. Decades of mass murder in the countryside. Liberals, Conservatives slitting each other's throats. He'd open the jails. 'The forgiving has to start somewhere,' he said, barely able to spit the words out. You had to admire. He lost in '61. In '65, he made the mistake of accepting communist support, and lost even the nomination."

Then, one night the rains came. Willi heard the drumming on the zinc roof and thought of the cistern filling, of the pigs having their baths again and becoming sleek.

The mountains turned green again in a matter of hours it seemed. The Virgin was saved, supposedly, but they all stopped looking up at her, and one day she wasn't there anymore.

On a day in the second week of December, just after the morning storm, one of the children of the storekeeper below came up with a message from Sonia: would *don* Will and *don* Carl come to her at the *abasto* without saying anything to anyone? They walked down the hill and found her alone in the little room behind the store:

"You will come with me and talk to him, please, un Norteamericano. They have kidnapped him and brought him to us," she said.

"What? Who?"

"Our people in the city. A rich *norteamericano*. He is a vice-president of a company. He is sick, dying maybe. It seems he wishes to die. You must talk to him. We cannot. He does not understand. You will see. There is a bus in an hour. You will return with me, and come back on the morning bus?"

"Yes, yes, of course," Willi said.

They sat and drank *aguardiente* in the chilly back room. There was a bus at eleven o'clock.

"We learned from the newspapers he is a diabetic," Sonia went on. "We have sent for insulin, a doctor. He has been in the *cordillera* for three weeks without insulin. It was too far. There were no doctors, so they brought him secretly to us. He is very weak; we must hurry. They are asking a quarter of a million dollars for his return. Our liaison says they are willing to pay. He is a vice-president, as I told you. The negotiations are going forward, but we must keep him alive."

"But what must we say to him?" Carl asked.

"That he must let the doctor examine him, test his urine, let us give him the injections, that his company wishes to pay the money.

"Always before we have returned these men alive. It is because of this they pay our ransoms."

The bus came. Sonia leaned close to speak in whispers: "It has never been our experience they die for their companies, you know. We don't know what is the matter with him. The doctor is risking much to come, but he is one of us."

They had given Paul Seybolt their bedroom. He lay on the cheap chenille spread, wearing chinos and a dirty tennis shirt. Willi sat on a bench at the far end of the little room. Carl stood in the doorway with Sonia.

"We speak English," Willi said.

The man said nothing.

Willi moved closer: "Why won't you let a doctor see you?"

"Good God!" laughed the man. "What next?"

"You're a diabetic?" Carl asked.

"So, you've been reading about me in the newspapers."

"We know they wish to return you alive, that things are going forward. Your company wishes to…"

"Who, precisely, are you?" Paul Seybolt said, looking at Carl.

"No one, really," Carl shrugged.

"What are you doing in this place?"

"A little of this and that," Willi said. "That's not the point."

"Ah, yes, 'No one really,' 'A little of this and that.' I have a son wants to be no one really. Sleep therapy, they're trying."

Seybolt lay with his eyes closed. He seemed to have exhausted himself. When he began speaking again had to come close to the bed.

"I was co-founder of this company they're demanding quarter of a million from; did the newspapers say that?"

"I don't know," Carl said. "We didn't see the papers."

"He will not eat," Sonia said. "He hasn't eaten for two days." There was perspiration
odor in the room, foot odor.

"Fourteen hour days we used to put in." Paul Seybolt found the strength to say. "I was worth a couple million then…

"Then, the big time. When we first came down here, company put us up in the Tucuman-Sheraton for four months while my wife searched for a house had enough style for us. You think that didn't cost …?"

"You're depressed," Willi said.

"Yes, depressed. Do you blame me? Let me finish. Even then, I was worth something to us. Then I had a heart attack; my son was put to sleep for three weeks to cure his maladjustment. We were in the hands of doctors. Pills to sleep, pills to wake up. Then my wife left me. I live alone in a twenty room house. Diminishing returns…"

"Your company wishes to pay."

"In the hands of doctors." The voice was weakening.

"Listen, man, they want to return you alive!" Willi shouted.

"They have their wants and I have mine," said Paul Seybolt, falling back on the pillow.

"You want to die?" Willi asked.

"Probably I do, yes." Seybolt took a couple deep breaths, then said, "Tell me, are you one of these?"

"We are friends," Willi said.

"Ah, friends. Yes. Yes, probably I will die. They chose the wrong man, tell them."

Carl went in the kitchen where Sergio was. "Can you have the injections given forcibly?"

"Perhaps. The pharmacist gave me a kit to test the urine."

"How soon can the money be found?"

"They are still negotiating."

They sat at the kitchen table and had meat pies with hot chocolate. The rain continued.

"I think there is more to treating him than just insulin," Sonia said. "I think there are matters about diet. He asks for *aguardiente* but will not eat."

Sonia cleared the table and set out a bottle of rum. The children worked on geometry problems at the foot of the table under the oil lamp. At about nine-thirty, the doctor came: a frightened man in his sixties. He had been contacted by telegram and had never before in his life received a telegram, he told them.

"Have you brought the insulin?" Sonia asked, serving him a cup of chocolate.

"Yes. I could hardly decipher the message. I was so flustered. Have you the urine? They told me they gave you a kit."

"Yes." Sonia brought the urine in a preserve jar. The doctor dipped a tape in it:

"You must do this twice a day. If the green patch turns brown, as you see here, increase the insulin injections. Then, this pink patch…if it darkens, there is a ketosis. You must give extra feedings. Who is to give the injection?"

"I," said Sonia.

"We can begin with forty units in the morning. If the patch turns brown, give another twenty in the evening." He mopped the sweat off his face. "I sincerely doubt you can handle this."

"We must handle it," said Sonia.

"He's four plus," the doctor said, comparing the little tab to a chart on the side of the bottle, "But no ketosis so far. Simply giving insulin is not the entire solution. You have insulin shock to avoid. He becomes weak and perspires, you must give sugar water and hold the injection."

"Yes, yes, I understand," Sonia said.

They went in the bedroom and held him down while the doctor observed Sonia give the injection. It was easy; there was no strength in him. The doctor examined his eyes and feet. There was an infected toenail. "That's bad. Use this Betadine solution I'll leave you."

They went back in the kitchen and Sonia offered the doctor an *empanada*. He waved it away. His stomach had been upset all day.

"A little cup of *manzanilla*?" Sonia offered.

"No no, nothing. This is serious, serious. It will have to be hurried up."

"There is nothing we can do," Sergio said. "It is a matter of currency. The money must be usable."

"Yes, yes, well I've done what I can do."

He picked up his bag. "Cannot come back. It is too dangerous."

The captive dozed.

"Perhaps it will be all right, if only he will eat. As long as he is so weak, we can handle the injections and the urine," Sonia said. "You must go now. No one must know. If we need you, I will send to the *abasto*."

They went back on the bus. No one had noticed their absence.

On Wednesday Willi went up. Seybolt looked thinner. His face was shiny with perspiration. "He will not eat," Sergio said.

"Sometimes when he wants the aguardiente very badly I can get him to eat a little soup before I let him drink," Sonia said.

"But it is not enough," said Sergio. "I called the doctor; he will send someone from the *Rurales* to put a nose tube."

"Tell him," Sonia said, "he will save himself the tubes if he will eat. You can tell him he will be tied down and very uncomfortable."

"I know, I know," said Seybolt, understanding her. "Let them do what they must. I'm too weak to fight them."

"The money is arranged," Sergio said. "It is only to take him to the meeting place. But it is far and he will not stand the trip as he is. We cannot show them a corpse."

"Why do you do this?" Willi said to the man on the bed. "Your disease can be controlled."

"My disease, yes. Try it yourself. I have the childhood type even though it started when I was thirty. You want to see the muscles in my legs?" He pulled up his pant leg. The thigh muscle was pulled up in a knot, as if no longer attached to the tendon and bone.

"Impotent too; you never knew that, did you, about diabetes? You think it's just a matter of a little insulin."

They brought the lentil soup that Sonia had on the stove, but he shook his head. Sergio gave him some guava juice with the aguardiente in it. "It will do him harm in the long run, but maybe in the short..."

Sergio poured them all a drink.

"So you do a little 'this and that?'" Seybolt said, looking a little revived.

"Yes; we farm a little," Willi said.

"What do you grow?"

"Pepper, beans, corn."

Seybolt sat up. "Have to pee."

They helped him up. He stood weakly, with Willi's help, and urinated into a pail in the corner. Sonia dipped one of the tapes in the urine. Negative. She frowned. There was a slight ketosis. Seybolt started to fall coming back to the bed. Will caught him, helped him zip up his fly.

"They pee like any other *miserable*," said Sergio, "these vice presidents."

The afternoon rain had begun. Sonia put bowls under two leaks. A man in a poncho came to the door. Sergio went out in the yard to talk to him.

"We have the Jeep," Sergio said to Sonia when he came back in. "We start next Monday. They will send someone this afternoon with the nose tube and the Similac. Tell him this," Sergio said to Carl, "And ask him once more if he will eat."

Willi shook Seybolt awake and explained about the nose tube. The man's skin felt loose on his bones,

"Give me more *aguardiente*."

They gave him the *aguardiente* in milk this time, and he spat it out.

They waited, drinking Cruz Verde now. Seybolt slept, perspiring in spite of the chill. The rain stopped and the sun shone briefly in through the shutters, then it was dark. They put off eating. "He must be here soon," Sergio said. "Or I will have to go."

A boy of sixteen or so finally came at nearly six-thirty with a nose tube and three cans of Similac.

"And the student?" Sonia asked.

"He's been arrested."

"But why? He's done nothing…?"

"It will be as an example," said Sergio. "They know whoever has the Gringo will be looking for medical help. The student attended meetings."

"Do you know how to insert the tube?" Sonia asked the boy hopelessly.

"I know nothing,"

Sergio was taking down his poncho from the nail. He would go for the midwife in the next village.

"Go, *mijo*," Sonia said. "He is dying. I feel it."

The schoolbooks were pushed to one end of the table, and they sat down in the kitchen and had the soup and fried plantains. "Perhaps it's lucky they arrested him," Sonia said. "They might have let him lead them to us."

"Pig!" Willi jumped up and stood in the bedroom door: "Pig!" he shouted at the sleeping man. "You'll let these people be your murderers!"

Seybolt opened his eyes.

"These are good, decent people. They don't want you to die!"

Seybolt wiped his face on the sheet. "Give me *aguardiente.*"

"No *aguardiente*! Soup. You will drink soup! Bring it!" He gestured to Sonia. She brought a cup of the thick broth.

"Good people, and you will destroy them!" Willi shouted. Sonia handed him the cup. "Drink, now!" He held the cup to the sick man.   "Drink!"

Seybolt drank and gagged.

"Drink!" Willi yelled. But Seybolt pushed the cup away. "Tube down your nose. You want that?"

Seybolt lay on the bed, weakened and gasping; but shaking his head, "No, no…!" They left him and went back in the kitchen. Our nerves are giving out, Willi thought. He'd better come, he'd better come soon.

They sat, silent, listening.to the beetles bump against the shutters. A parade of them came in under the door and crossed the room and went out again under the back door. "We built in their path," Sonia said. "Now they come through any way they can or knock themselves dead trying. Every morning I sweep them up."

After they had finished eating," Sonia and the girl washed up the dishes. The boy sat at the; table cleaning the chimneys of the oil lamps. "You should be in bed," Sonia said without her usual conviction, so they stayed up.

"These will be different," Sonia said after a while. "These will be a doctor and an engineer."

"*Ay, mami, ya no!*"

"Yes, the boy a doctor, the girl an engineer. It is decided. They are excellent students. They will have scholarships if God pleases.

"They are each top in their examinations. They will go to the technical school at Los Olmos and to the *Nacional.* Those who finish in the top three at the technical are given full scholarships."

"*Ya basta Mami!*"

"Listen, don Willi, listen! You two be quiet; you two have nothing to do with this! If anything happens next week…"

"*Que va a pasar, Mami!*"

"The *Doña,* go to The *Doña.* They are innocent children. She will understand that."

"Yes, yes, of course," Willi said.

"My brother's address . . . here, here!" She pulled a trunk out from under a daybed in the corner of the kitchen, opened it and took out a leatherette box which contained a stack of letters. "Here." Taking a blank envelope, she wrote two addresses. "My brother, who lives in Pellicer, and my sister-in-law in the capital. The *Doña* will see they are sent to one or the other."

"Of course, of course."

"I have told them to run to the cave up there and hide. They will wait for you there."

"Yes, yes."

"A doctor and an engineer. You will remember."

Sergio came back alone at about eight thirty.

"She would not come!" Sergio said. "She demonstrated to me its use."

They sat the gringo up and tied his hands behind his back. Sonia sat on his legs and Willi grasped him around the chest. Sergio held the tube up to the light of the oil lamp hung over the bed and blew up a little balloon at the end.

"If he would swallow it, it would be simple; but since he certainly won't, it must be inserted through the nose. Miller-Abbot tube," he murmured with satisfaction, applying Vaseline and deflating the bulb at the end. "The little balloon is blown up when the thing is in place and the intestine moves it along. Hold him now."

Paul Seybolt shook his head violently, but Willi grasped it.

"Oopa, it's in!" Sergio said, threading it rapidly down, noting the gradations. Then it stopped.

"Not far enough," Sergio frowned. "This mark must pass the nostril."

Paul Seybolt had become very still.

"He's closing off the gullet. I can feel it." Sergio pulled out the tube.

"Give him *aguardiente,*" Willi said. They held the glass to his lips. He retched, drank.

"Let him rest a bit." Sergio wiped his face on his sleeve.

"He's very drunk," Sonia said. "I don't like his color. Try again."

They sat him up again. He was almost dead weight this time. The tube went down. "If only we haven't killed him with *aguardiente*." Sonia got the Similac and attached a funnel to the end of the tube. While Sergio held it up, she poured the gruel in.

"Is it going down?"

"Maybe. You've made it too thick."

"I followed the directions on the can."

"There, there it goes. He held the tube higher.

"Something to hold it; I can't much longer," Sergio said.

"The mosquito net, tie it to the…"

That worked well. Sergio gave the funnel to Willi and found some rubber bands Taking his belt, he hung the buckle off the hook; then, with the rubber bands, he fastened the funnel to the lower end of the belt.

Sonia stood on a chair to fill the funnel every few minutes or so. "It goes faster now," she said. Paul Seybolt was asleep and snoring, but his color seemed better.

"I thought we were lost. Maybe we are lost. He'll revive. But will we get him to Las Cruces? It's six hours by Jeep," Sergio said.

"It made me itch to 'throw down my shovel and go out there and shoulder a rifle with Chu Teh,'" Willi told Carl when he got back.

"What?" said Carl.

"You won't guess who said that."

"Who?"

"Uncle Joe Stilwell. After Chiang sent him home, just before the whole Nationalist façade came down to the tune of billions invested. One of these remarks almost got him in trouble with McCarthy."

"Who was Chu Teh?"

"One of Mao's guys. Uncle Joe was one of my dad's heroes. Vinegar Joe. He loved the Chinese soldier, saw how the Communists cared for their own. He even went up there and saw them. Big, healthy guys, trained, cared for. And he saw how Chiang never even noticed things like his people were starving, soldiers left to die on the field, while he worried about a shipment of watermelons.

"'Agrarian reformers,' Uncle Joe called them.

"Sonia asked me to have these people here help the children if anything happens. But, better wait to see if it's necessary."

In the big house they prepared *Nochebuena*. The *Doña* gathered moss, brought out the bark stable, the porcelain holy family—the Child and the Magi left hidden in excelsior until the last. On the day of the *Iluminación*, the first of the nine candles was lit and family, servants, the three gringos gathered before The *Doña's* nativity scene, which took up a whole end of the verandah; a sandy plain with little oases made of real plants and moss.

And each night The *Doña* read one of the nine prayers: *"Bendita eres entre mujeres, Y bendito el fruto…"* while don Rafa smoked in the courtyard set off *estrellitas*, little sticks of gunpowder, tossing them in a high arc over the plantains. Eight days, seven days; the porcelain kings began their journey over the mossy plain. The beasts waited, stolid, and Orlando's wife, too, waited heavily on her knees:

"Bendita eres entre mujeres y bendito el fruto de tu vientre, Jesús."

Berta's husband came from the city. He was a quiet man. When the children bothered him he went out to hoe in the garden.

"Another Christmas," don Rafa remarked to Carl one day in Tuxpan. "How time goes. As Ortega y Gasset said somewhere, 'If life were a toothache that would be an advantage.'"

"Carl had finished his grocery shopping and Rafa had replenished his little supply of fireworks, so they walked together to the Café Media Luna. It would rain any minute.

Don Rafa ordered two glasses of rum.

"Oh, by the way, there are things known about them up there, your friends," he said.

"Who?"

"Sergio Molina and his wife. Evidently they are connected with the holding of a wealthy industrialist."

"How did you know!"

"Why in *El Mundo* of course."

"*El Mundo!*" It hadn't occurred to Carl any of the matters they had witnessed those two rainy afternoons up on the mountain could find their way into a newspaper.

But of course they would. Seybolt's kidnapping had been news for weeks before they met him. How could they have been so stupid not to watch the papers! How could they have simply gone back to their chores and expected to one day go up there and find Sonia and Sergio back at their coffee beans and the children at their geometry…!"

"They are among a group of suspects. What do you know for a fact?"

"Well, nothing. Sergio organizes strikes. That's all we know. Your wife also knows that." Should he perhaps confide in this man, Carl wondered. Could he help? He noted Rafa giving a slow survey of a young woman sitting at a table nearby and decided not.

"It is said the poor wretch is presumed to be half dead with sugar.

"And that he is hidden somewhere around here."

"Of that we heard nothing. Willi likes to go up there and talk about the soil with Sergio."

The mangos ripened and the margaritas bloomed extravagantly; the garden in riot after the rains.

The fourth night before *Nochebuena* the pregnant child knelt heavily in the candlelight, and Olga from the kitchen sang a barbarous carol from Chocotán accompaied by the nephews banging pan lids. *Don* Rafa shared a bottle of Cruz Verde with Luciano. They set off two *volcanes,* which sputtered down the hillside into the cane.

A bat woke Blanche at four. She heard Orlando's whistle, went out on the stoop.

"*Hola,*" he said, coming into the light of the lantern in his kitchen. "What's the matter?"

"There's a bat."

"You want coffee?"

She went and sat on his steps. He came out with two tin cups.

"What's the matter?"

"Nothing. A bat."

"You don't get enough loving maybe?"

"Maybe."

"You tell Orlando about it."

"You're on your rounds."

"I'll just whistle a minute." He blew a blast.

"Why do you whistle? To warn the thieves?"

He laughed. "*Vigilantes* must whistle. Otherwise their employers might think they are sleeping… Some loving, eh?" He moved closer to her, kissed the side of her neck.

"And your rounds?"

"You wait. I go?"

"No."

"Come with me then."

"All right."

At the top of the pasture he blew a blast on his whistle, and then spread his poncho under one of the silkcotton trees that marked the division between the The *Doña's* property and the *Franceses*. She sat down on it and pulled her own poncho around her. He sat next to her and traced a finger along her jaw.

"Funny girl."

"It's cold."

"I warm you. Tell me something."

"What?"

"You sleep with him too?"

"Who?"

"The other one."

"Willi? No. Funny, us talking English."

"I love the English. I go back there so quick I have a chance. You take me, eh?"

"We aren't going back. It's crazy. You all want to go there."

"Sure we would go! All of us would go, every miserable son of a *puta*," he said. "Here there is nothing. *Nada!*"

"But you're married," Blanche said.

"That is The *Doña*. That is no matter. She belong here. I send her something. Here, sit closer; take this off here."

He pulled off her poncho and her sweater, and lay beside her, his leg astride her legs. "Beautiful, beautiful. *Don* Carl, I bet he don't appreciate you."

"He did once."

He pulled up her nightgown and pinched her breasts.

"It's *her* he loves, you know."

"Who?" he undid his pants.

"The old woman."

"The *Doña?*"

"Yes."

Orlando was shocked. "But she wouldn't ever…"

"Of course not. It's impossible. That's why he likes it."

He got up: "I'll just whistle…"

"Hurry. It's cold."

"Hurry, she says, the little woman. Yes yes, I hurry." He blew a blast and crawled back to the blanket: "He is coming, your Orlando, coming."

Carl went alone up the mountain. He found the children at the outdoor table with their homework, and Sonia among the drying coffee beans. The Jeep had not come, but *El Vicepresidente* was still alive. Sergio had got the knack of the nose tube. It was worrisome, yes, that their district and some of their associates were being named in the papers.

"But we go on, *don* Carl," said Sonia. "We have a crop ready," she indicated the burlap drop cloths covered with ripe coffee beans spread all about her.

Carl told her about Rafa's suspicions.

"Oh, he will never harm us; but it is best to keep from him what we can. We will be discreet. Don't come again unless I send for you."

"But how will we know?" Carl asked.

"There are the newspapers."

"No, we will come, one of us, when we can."

"All right. You are very good to us. The *Doña* will help if there is need. I have given directions to *don* Willi. The children…"

The morning of *Nochebuena*, the *carnicero* came to the farm up the hill to kill the pig. Carl heard the squeals at five in the morning; he got up. Willi was up already in the kitchen. "Hurry," he said, "I want to see all of this." They climbed the hill behind the stable.

Clouds covered the slopes, rolling through the coffee bushes and eucalyptus trees. They climbed up a slippery path, catching at the clumps of *argentina* grass. The sun was just behind the *cordillera*; thin rays broke through the pile of purple clouds which would bring the day's storm. At the top of the field they climbed up to the stone steps below *Los Frances* brick bungalow. On the patio at a long table covered with oil cloth *doña* Eulalie, her two servants, and their own Olga and Miriam sat chopping messes of cilantro and green onions. Out behind the house, Luciano and the *carnicero* stood in the stable, waiting for the blood of the drawn pig to collect in an aluminum washtub. Just outside, Orlando had built a fire with an improvised spit from which two large kettles were hung. The carcass was skinned and the head cut off and thrown in the boiling water. The steaming intestines were pulled out and washed under the spigot. *Doña* Eulalia brought out the wooden bowls full of chopped herbs and dumped them into the congealing blood in the aluminum tub. This mixture was then ladled into the tied-off gut to make blood sausage. These were boiled in the pot with the head. Next the fatback was removed and sent into the kitchen to be fried for breakfast. Eight o'clock by now, the clouds were lifting. Glittering droplets condensed on the plantains and coffee bushes. Carl and Willi fed the fire with dead wood. *Doña* Luz arrived; Olga brought out hot chocolate, and they sat on milking stools to drink.

The *carnicero* went to work then, stretching the carcass on a platform of rough boards. He hacked off the trotters, which went into the pot, then cut off the two haunches. Eulalia had a huge wooden vat filled with salt water and nitrate ready to receive these. The loins, with the bone removed, were stretched out in long wooden troughs and covered with the same onions and cilantro that had gone into the sausage; then a mixture of beer and orange juice was poured over them. "These will go in the oven tonight," Eulalia explained to Willi, who was copying down the recipes in a notebook.

The gray clouds piled up like dirty linen, and the wind rose, rattling the leathery plantain leaves. Luciano rigged a tarpaulin over the fire and the woodpile. The sausages were fished out, and Olga carried some of them off to fry in the kitchen. The salivating dogs hung about and were thrown bits of gristle and bone. Thunder rolled; it grew dark, and fat raindrops pattered on the zinc roof of the stable. A child dressed as a pirate ran out of the house:

"*Está servido.*"

They left the fire and went in to sit at the long table at the end of the patio. Olga and Miriam brought plates of *chicharrones*, sausages, and fried plantains. Rain poured off the tiles. "Eat up," said *don* Jorge. "It will have to last you till midnight."

The great bruised clouds raced overhead; suddenly a white sun broke through. The patter slowed; the drains gurgled. An almond *turrón* was brought and sliced with little cups of black coffee. Miriam, looking wan, cleared the table. Eulalia went to baste the meat. *Don* Rafa took aguardiente to the *carnicero*; and *don* Jorge offered Will and Carl cigars.

"What a lot of work," *don* Jorge said, stretching out in a hammock. "My wife gives herself this trouble twice a year. There're plenty of beds, anyone wants a nap."

A series of dark bedrooms opened off the patio. Carl found a small room with an iron bedstead. Two army blankets were folded at the bottom of the bed. He wrapped himself in one of these and fell into the deep sleep that the heavy blankets seemed to induce. In another room, Eulalia's daughter slept beside her suckling child. Rafa slept on an army cot and his wife on Eulalia's big iron bed. The *carnicero* dozed on a bench in the stable.

Carl, waking in the dark room felt stupefied with food and sleep. He went to the spigot and washed his face. Work had begun again. The gelatinous liquid in the kettles was poured through a strainer into five long tin molds; then, what was left behind in the strainer was picked through and the bones thrown to the dogs. The rest: brains, tongue, trotters, chopped fine and stirred into the gelatin. The dying fire was built up again, and one of the hindquarters spitted to roast. The *carnicero* had gone, taking with him a side of fatback, his payment.

Luciano tended the meat, basting it with *habanera*, which caused the flames to leap. Rafa had brought out a bottle of *aguardiente*.

"Gives herself this trouble when we could have stuck it all in a freezer down in the city," said don Jorge.

"Used to keep it all salted before the hydroelectric. Didn't taste like much," said Rafa. "Smelled to heaven. Luciano here would remember. You remember how we used to keep meat before the hydroelectric?"

"Yes. My father would smoke it."

"How long would it keep?" Willi asked. "Weeks? Months?"

"More like weeks."

"Troublesome beasts," said Jorge. "I remember I was living in the capital, one of my clerks brought me a pig up the elevator, presented it to me for *Nochebuena*. I had to give half of it to the swindler at the butcher's in order to get it taken care of."

"One thing you can say for up here in the mountains, the *carnicero* takes his side of fatback and a bottle of Cruz Verde and considers himself well paid," said *don* Rafa. The nephews and two of Eulalia's grandchildren had dressed themselves up as pirates and cowboys and were throwing *estrellitas* into the coffee bushes. The sun dropped behind the *cordillera*, and some rockets from Kilómetro Veinticinco burst among the eucalyptus trees. Orlando and *don* Alberto made several trips bringing gifts, salads, two roasted chickens.

Don Rafa opened a bottle of Cruz Verde and sliced up a green mango. He and Jorge had begun their serious drinking and didn't touch the bits of Genoa sausage and white cheese, the cups of bread soup that were sent around. The children seemed drunk to Carl, reeling about as harlequins, Cinderellas, pirates. But he realized it must be a phenomenon of his own drunkeness. The little girls tripped on the hems of their long dresses: "Papa, give us *estrellitas*."

"Papa. When does *el Niño* come?"

At midnight, *mijo*," said his father, who was hoeing calmly in *don* Jorge's garden. Carl took some soup and closed his eyes to steady the world.

"Come," Orlando said to Blanche, pulling her into the trees. "There's no one below."

They slipped and slid down the hillside. He had a bottle of *habanera* with him, which he passed her. "My girl," he said, slipping his hand under her poncho and into her shirt. "No one care if I whistle tonight, eh?" He pinched her breast. She drank the rum, shivering:

"It's cold."

"Warm in my place," he said. "Oven's been on all day."

"Not there."

"Yes, in the bed." They felt their way around behind the stable and through the plantain grove. He lit a match. "Come quick!" He found the lantern and lit it, bringing it into the kitchen and setting it on the floor. He unwrapped her poncho, started on her buttons. Her bowels felt watery. He took off her shirt, undid the waist of her jeans, pulled them down and ran his hands over her belly: beautiful, beautiful."

"Sick," she murmured and ran out to the porch and vomited. He came out behind her.

"Oh, Christ, I hate being sick! Go away!"

"*Ahora sí, ahora sí.*" He held her while she hung over retching; then she had to run to the latrine. He followed her with the lantern, stood over her while her bowels turned to water. "Now, now, it passes," leading her back to the bedroom. "Better now, better now, yes."

She lay across the bed. He rubbed her, kissed her all over. "I have you here. I have you in all the beds, in The *Doña's...*"

"Oh, no! God!" She felt better.

"A little drink, just a little." He passed her the bottle. She drank, coughed. He slipped off his clothes, lay beside her, stroked her pale, inner arms: "*Tan blanca que es, doña Blanca...*

"We must go up. I have a bad feeling," Carl said.

"Later. When they begin the firecrackers, and the women are praying." Willi said.

Bursts of red and green rose over Kilómetro Treinta. "Big doings in Kilómetro Treinta tonight," said Jorge, "Luz Marina Rosano was named Queen of the Sugarcane."

"The girl from Zacapa?"

"She was born in Tuxpan. It was on the radio they've turned over the Brigadier's Jeep and there's been a stabbing. A character in a *cantina* said she had silicone breasts."

"What a thing to say about one ofó our women. Silicone, breasts!"

Olga sent word from the kitchen that the pregnant child had stomach cramps.

"Probably too much turrón," said Berta; she told Olga to have her lie down. "Her time isn't for three weeks yet." She wiped soot from the face of her youngest.

"Is the *Niño* coming?" he asked his mother.

"Not for another couple hours."

"Where is Orlando?" asked *doña* Luz

"He's taken himself off somewhere. Probably Kilómetro Treinta."

"*Now* is the *Niño* coming?"

"But *mijo,* it's only two minutes since you asked," said Berta. "Do you know your piece? Say your piece for me."

"*Mambrú se fue a la guerra*
Que dolor, que dolor, que pena.
Mambrú se fue a la guerra.
No se si volverá…"

the child shouted, and ran away.

At eleven thirty the younger children were sent to try to bring the men inside without success. They still had the big rockets to throw.

"It is quarter to twelve. We must pray without them," said Luz, leading the children and servants into the verandah.

"But the rockets…," said the nephews, torn.

"The *Niño* cannot come until we pray," said Berta, pushing the children into the room. Carl stood with *don* Alberto in the dark entryway, hovering, between men's affairs and women's. The *Doña* read the prayers for the last day. One exhausted child lay in her lap. The older children knelt in the front, their faces on a level with Eulalia's rustic stable and its porcelain figures. Behind stood the servants, their faces lit by the flickering candles. The pregnant child crouched off to one side, clutching her belly.

The *Doña* finished her reading, and Berta's heavy voice began the Salve Maria's, rising and falling monotonously.

Miriam groaned and The *Doña* went to her and led her from the room. He wondered where Blanche was. He supposed she might be asleep in one of the bedrooms.

"*La torre está en guardia*
La torre está en guardia.
Quien la destruirá?"

The children sang, and don Alberto looked at his watch. "Midnight," he said.

"*El Niño!*" the children shouted. Eulalia, feeling under the skirts of the table, brought out the porcelain figure, which she placed in the straw.

The children, revived from their stupor, tore at the wrappings of the gifts, which were passed out by Berta and Eulalia. "Calmly, calmly!" scolded *doña* Luz, but she was ignored.

The haunch was brought in, and saffron rice, baked plantains, roast chicken, fried yucca, *tamales* wrapped in banana leaves, fruit salad. The children, revived by their toys, paid little attention to food, and *don* Rafa and *don* Jorge still refused to come in.

No one will know."

Orlando put the lantern down on the floor of the big bedroom. Blanche stood in the doorway, saw herself from the waist up in the big mirror above the dressing table.

"Come." He lay on his back on The *Doña's* bed, waiting. "They are all up there above. How can they know we are here?"

"Why must we?" she said. "Why must we in this room?"

"Because you're my lady," he said. "My *doña* Blanca. Come." He held out the bottle.

She drank.

"Lie down here by me."

"No." She held the blanket around her.

"I told you. They are all up there. The men are drunk and the women are praying."

"Turn out the light then."

He turned down the wick. She went to him. Now I am lost, she thought.

When the eating was over and people starting to go home, Miriam was discovered bent over the kitchen sink. "*Diós Santo*! Where is Orlando?" cried Berta. He was discovered coming up the hill and sent to take the girl home and fetch Solita.

Carl found Blanche alone on the dark verandah. "What's the matter?"

"Nothing."

"Didn't you want to eat?"

"I…"

"What is it?"

"Something awful's happening."

"To you?"

"To us."

"Where've you been?"

"I went to lie down."

"Are you sick?"

"Yes."

It was three in the morning when they went down the mountain. Orlando was gone off on his bicycle. The girl moaned softly in the back room of the hut. The children were carried off to bed. Luciano and Rafa smoked in the courtyard, finishing off a bottle of Cruz Verde. Carl sat on the stoop. Blanche had gone to bed. Willi came in and put on fresh clothes. "I'm going up."

"Go, Yes, go!"

Willi stood in the doorway of the cottage. There were no signs of Christmas here. Sonia sat at the table, and he could see through the doorway that the Similac bottle still hung from the hook that held the mosquito net.

"Nothing," said Sonia. We do not hear. We had a message two days ago they were to come this morning with a Jeep. We have waited all day."

"Not even a message?"

"Nothing. Sit. Sergio sleeps. I am watching.

"Something has happened. Don Willi, Sergio and I will go with the *Americano* if the Jeep comes. But the children are to hide in the cave until we've left. Then they will go to Solita and she will send word to you.

"They are to go to my brother. They are to study and receive scholarships. She must be firm in this, for they do not listen to me..."

Willi frowned. He could think of nothing to say.

"Perhaps it is not necessary. You can wait some days. If we do not return..."

"I will take them now. Let me take them now."

"No, they would not go. They are serious children, and good. We must respect their wishes in this. They will hide when the Jeep comes and then run to Solita."

"You should come now, with them. Let Sergio go!"

"I cannot, *don* Willi. You know what I am. What we are."

"Tell me then. If we have no word, and you are gone. Who then?"

"Who?"

"Who then I go to?" Willi reverted to pidgin speech when he talked to Sonia.

"I tell you that and you become too involved, you are in danger like us."

"Tell me more."

"Aye, *don* Willi!"

"Tell me more."

"The pharmacist at Kilómetro Treinta."

"*Que no aguantooooo!*" groaned the girl

"So it begins, does it," said Rafa.

"Will it be long?" Willi asked.

"Could be a day or more."

"Noooooooooo! *Que me mata!*"

Willie walked outside of the circle of lamplight. The girl was moving about. Something fell
over in the cottage. "I'll take her some rum," said Rafa, going in with the bottle.

It became quiet, and Willi fell asleep for a time in a hammock.

Nearly dawn. The mist rose in tatters. The girl was screaming; Orlando still not returned. Carl sat on the porch holding his head. *Don* Rafa came out in slippers.

"The old woman will be with another," he said. "Ah, well, it's better without her, I've always felt. I never liked Solita with her injections, putting the infant to sleep, so it forgets to breathe. Olga is up; she will go over."

Something heavy fell over in the hut; the girl shuffled from room to room, bumping into the furniture.

"Mongrel bitch I had once," said Rafa, "…ran in circles, dropping her litter here and there. Red as a fox. Dropped one of her whelps in my shoe."

"*Nooooo!*" the girl bellowed, "*Ni un momento mas!*"

"*Aguanta pues, si no hay remedio,*" said Rafa. "In my day they delivered themselves hanging from a rope tied to the rafters. In hammocks too; that was a trick. No, better without Solita and her ampules. I'm not the only man to say it. It doesn't do to ask the women. You don't ask a woman to be objective."

"*Uy, uy, uy.*"

Something else fell over and broke. Willi went to the spigot and ran some cold water over his face. The patio was filled with a silvery half light.

"*No, no, no NO!*"

He found a bottle of Ron Viejo and took it over to the other hut. The girl was crouched in a corner of the kitchen, her eyes wild.

"Have this," he said, holding out the bottle, "*Tenga.*"

She wouldn't get up. He found a glass on the floor, filled it and took it to her. She drank it, choked. He gave her more. She drank it, then settled in a heap, moaning. "I'll stay with you, shall I?" Willi said, righting a chair and sitting down. She stared at him. He was speaking English without thinking. Then she began screaming: "No, no, no!"

"You want me to leave?"

She got up and began running again, stumbling over the debris on the floor. He backed out: "I'll get Olga," he said. "You must have someone. Yes, I'll get Olga…"

Olga came out, and The *Doña*, with armfuls of linen. "It won't be yet," Olga said after she had settled the girl in bed. "The child is high in the womb. She is frightened is all. She is young."

A pale bicycle light wavered below on the road, turned the corner and came slowly up. Orlando walked the bicycle, a figure beside him, wrapped in a blanket.

"She was with someone else," Orlando said. Solita was an ageless Indian with a gray blanket thrown over her shoulders. She carried a worn briefcase. Orlando led her into the hut. "*Basta*," she said to the moaning girl; "You be quiet." Her dark figure moved about in front of the lamp.

"She'll give her an injection," Rafa said. "She'll settle her."

Willi made coffee. They sat at the table on the porch as the sky lightened. Orlando came out of the hut and sat on the stoop. "It'll be hours," she says.

"*Sí, hombre.* What kept you?"

"She was with a woman in La Florida. There was a hemorrhage."

"Women," said don Rafa. "I have one volcán left. We'll set it off when your son is born."

"Yes, man!"

"Right off the cliff there, over Kilómetro Veinticinco." Don Rafa walked over to the edge of the courtyard and set up the little rocket. "For the little president, eh? That's why Orlando came back to this place where Judas lost his boots. So his son can be native born, eligible for the presidency, eh?"

"Oh sure!" said Orlando.

"*Uy!*" moaned the girl, "*Uy!*"

"*Te callas, te callas, oye,*" from Solita.

"Have their ways of killing here, too," Blanche murmured behind Carl in the doorway, where she sat.

"*Not a place for us, Carl. It's death. I feel it.*"

"*Uy! Uy! Uy!*"

"You told her to give her a sedative?" Rafa asked Orlando. "Solita doesn't let them scream for long."

"*Fucking talk!*"

"*Fucking...!*"

Rafa turned around to look at Blanche: "*Pero, doña* Blanche..."

"Fuck you, fuck you all, fuck you all!" Carl grabbed her, held her from behind.

"Fucking, fucking, fucking, fucking . . .!"

She is hysterical. It has been too much. We will go in," said Rafa. "We will go to bed; there is nothing we can do out here."

Solita was sent over to give Blanche an injection. She slept and woke, slept and woke. Dreamed of giving birth to a small monkey.

They got up at noon. It was quiet. Willi found Rafa smoking in the garden.

"How goes it?"

"Labor stopped. Solita is letting her rest. Later, she will give quinine to start it again."

"All over again?"

"Yes. A dangerous thing."

The ladies came to play hearts and eat *turrón*, but Blanche didn't go over. She was curled up on the big iron bed, moaning. At times her moans repeated the timbre and rhythm of the moans that came from next door; for the quinine had been administered and labor had resumed. Carl sat at the foot of the bed trying to read. He wanted to touch Blanche, but she wouldn't let him.

Willi hoed in the beans, to put to some use the restlessness in his muscles that wanted to take him up the mountain. The moans rose and fell, but the exhaustion of the previous night, the repetition of something already lived, took the urgency out of them.

At eight that evening, the child, a boy, was born dead.

"So," said Rafa, coming out from the big house to where they sat on the stoop. "*El Presidentito* is dead. The little President is dead…

"This one in there," he shrugged a shoulder toward Orlando's hut. "This one might have been a little president…little brown president to promise holidays to the workers, yes…"

Carl went in to Blanche. She was up and dressed. "I'm leaving," she said. She had on her Boston Common polo shirt.

And then it was on the radio that Rafa kept in the stable. The holders of the kidnapped executive had been taken in.

"A Jeep was sent and they were all taken to the capital, Rafa told Willi.

"Yes," Willi said in anguish. "They were expecting it to take them to to Purua," he confessed to Rafa. What was the good of concealing things from him any longer?

"Oh God! Oh, God! We thought everything would be all right. How, how?"

"A Jeep was sent; but it was sabotaged. Someone had talked. Two government agents were along."

"And are they killed? Sonia …!"

"Sergio's in prison. The woman and children I don't know. Arms were found…"

"Yes, yes, there were guns. We saw them."

"You were very foolish to go there."

"They were good people."

"I imagine they were."

"Did the man die? "

"He is said to be near death."

"Oh, God! It wasn't them. Himself, he killed himself. They tried to save him."

"A bad diabetic, the papers say."

"Yes. He refused to eat. They sent to the Rurales for a doctor after they had trouble getting

him to eat. No one would come. They sent a boy with a nose tube, Sergio put it in himself."

"And you?"

"We couldn't do anything. We were supposed to talk him into wanting to live. His mind was made up. His wife had left him. His son was some kind of misfit. I guess we reminded him of the son. We were worse than useless. And he was already very ill."

"An unhappy event all around. This Sergio will be shot; and others too, whether they helped or not. There will be examples made. It won't do their cause much harm. They're purposely decentralized. That's probably why no one would help."

"The children . . . We promised Sonia, the children! They were to hide where the arms…"

"They found the arms. They won't be there. You won't find them. This is a more serious matter than you appear to realize. Arms were found. A North American is dead, or almost."

But they went. They had to see. They had to wait three days as the rains were so hard and steady the road washed out. When they got there, they found no one, and the house was burned.

They walked around it, kicking in the ashes. Evidently it had been torched at the side where the bedrooms were. That part was fallen in; but the fire had burned out, leaving the kitchen intact. There were the two mattresses still on the floor, and the pot of soup and kettle of coffee on the kerosene stove. The children's books and papers were still at the end of the table where the girl had sat; and the two oil lamps the boy had been cleaning.

They climbed the hill at the back. The boards with the branches stapled to them were thrown about, and the crates pulled out and overturned. Books and weapons were gone. *Gorky's La Madre* lay face down in the mud. A dirty child watched them.

"Did they take all of them," Carl asked.

"*Sí, en un Jeep.*"

Blanche was on the steps with the backpacks when they got back. She was going as far as Tuxpan in the car with *don* Alberto, then on to the capital in *por puesto*.

A priest had come, was inside the hut with The *Doña*, praying. Orlando was in the plantain grove hammering together a coffin of palo santo.

Don Rafa had brought out a bottle of tequila, poured out three glasses: "Never forget they used to bottle it in the same bottle as their cattle purge. Dozens of accidents. Ah, well you've heard that story…"

"She has to go, Willi, you see that?" Carl said to Willi.

"She's sick. She's had too much. 'It's death,' she said; 'There's death here.' She started saying it a month ago, when the hens were dying, now this…"

"Of course. It's their ways, Carl. There's an ancient balance."

Carl could hear the murmured *Salve Marias* from the cottage, and see the shadowy figure of Luz moving about the bed. The child was lying on the kitchen table, he could see, on top of a white tablecloth. The priest's voice was a rumbling counter bass.

"Unfortunate, what's happened, but she'll have another," said Rafa. "Strong girl like her, how she did yell."

After it was all over, they found that Orlando was also gone.

Carl continued to care for the cow. Milking, took him twice as long as it had Orlando, and he also fed and hosed down the sow.

His daytime chores were usually done by noon, when he took a shower and changed into clean clothes that Orlando's woman brought in and put on his bed every day. One of the reasons she was shy and confused around him, he decided, was that he spent all his afternoons at the big house, as if he had been a guest from the city. It was as if his slopping around with the pig was some sort of aberration only a gringo would indulge in.

She did little things like hanging a curtain in his kitchen, and when there were embers from her woodstove on baking day, she would fill the old fashioned iron with them and press one of his better shirts as if to nudge him up to the level where he belonged.

The *Doña* had finished the Henry Adams and they began reading *Bleak House* in the week before they left for the city.

Then Willi moved up to Sonia's place.

After Carl had done his shopping in Tuxpan, Mondays, he continued on the bus, past the *abasto*, up the mountain to the margin of the farm where Willi was living in an outbuilding. There were only a few items that Willi needed from the town. A carton of Polar Beer, one pack of cigarettes—he smoked one cigarette each evening—salt, matches. For the rest, Willi had Sonia's chickens and the vegetable garden.

"Any news," Carl would ask, and there would be a hint by way of the pharmacist that the children had found their way to a caretaking family, of a plan being conceived. Finally there was confirmed information of another kidnapping in a distant province, intended as a swap for the mother's freedom. Sergio would never be freed.

Willi was holding the property together for Sonia. Weeding her garden and keeping her hens and harvesting some coffee which Carl would eventually sell in Tuxpan and the money would be put into an account for Sonia to have when she was free.

And he had found clay in the cut the backhoe had carved out of the mountainside to link up a new farmhouse to the main road. He showed it to Carl, wonderful shades of terra cotta and cream and lilac shoveled into plastic tubs; and a pile of sunbaked bricks, he was making in a wooden mold. First he would build a wood fired oven with these bricks, then he would fire bricks to build a proper kiln. He would build himself a studio then and make sculptures from the same clay, the idea of them already in his head.

"Like the first man," Carl had said.

"Yeah, soon I won't need the cigarettes. I'm weaning myself."

A week in March the family came back for a week.

"That flan has a nice face," said don Rafa, wiping the corners of his mouth, as Miriam removed the plates and Olga came behind with the tray of desserts.

"So, have you seen your painter friend?" he asked Carl.

Carl was cautious. "Not for a week."

"Is there any hope?" asked The *Doña*.

"Well, yes there might be," Carl said.

"We won't ask you for details," said Rafa. "And your friend?"

"He's harvesting Sergio's coffee," Carl said. "And living in an outbuilding."

Don Rafa had read of the new kidnapping in the newspaper, but Carl wouldn't be drawn into discussing it. Whatever its results, they would read of it in the paper. *Don* Rafa and The *Doña* would not be associated with anything Willi did in the future. Nor would Carl. He had told her one day as they walked on the garden paths about Sonia's request for her to help the children. Would she have done it. She had looked confused and said she would have had to think about it and take it up with the family.

The following day, she had turned her wonderful gaze on him and brought it up again.

Yes, she told him. She would have done it. And if Sonia is released someday, she will take her to herself.

One thing Carl wondered, as they continued *Bleak House* the next day, was if she had known that he and Blanche had not been married would she have made them marry, just as she had made Orlando marry Miriam. Probably not. They had still not been properly introduced at the time. Someday perhaps. Meanwhile he was watching.

Barbara de la Cuesta taught and worked as a journalist in South America, and has long been a teacher of English as a Second Language and Spanish. Out of this experience came her two prize winning novels, *The Spanish Teacher*, winner of the Gival Press Award in 2007, and *Rosa*, winner of the Driftless Novella Prize from Brain Mill Press in 2017. Fellowships in fiction from the Massachusetts Artists' Foundation, and the New Jersey Council on the Arts, as well as residencies at the Ragdale Foundation, The Virginia Center, and the Millay Colony, have allowed her to complete these novels. She has also published two collections of poetry with Finishing Line Press, and her collection of short stories, *The Place Where Judas Lost his Boots,* has recently won The Brighthorse Prize for short fiction.

CPSIA information can be obtained
at www.ICGtesting.com
Printed in the USA
JSHW041701141220
10251JS00002B/154